THE
WARRIOR
ANGEL

The
Warrior Angel

M.A. Beasley

Copyright © 2023 by M.A. Beasley

All rights reserved. No parts of this book may be used or reproducedby
any means, graphic, electronic, and mechanical, including
photocopying, recording, taping, or by any information storage
retrieval system, without the written permission of the publisher except
in the case of brief quotations embodied in critical articles and reviews.

ISBN: 979-8-9880718-0-8 (Paperback)
ISBN: 979-8-9880718-1-5 (E-book)

Library of Congress Control Number: 2023905836

Printed in the United States of America

Published by

Quippy Quill
info@thequippyquill.com
(302) 295-2278

ACKNOWLEDGEMENT

I would like to first of all thank my sister Karla for inspiring me to write a book in the first place. She has published two children's booksand is currently working on her own horror novel. She has helped me every step of the way from spitting ideas, covers, even titles. Thank you to my husband Jon, daughter Shelby, and son Jonathan for supporting and giving me encouragement. Also, much gratitude to everyone at the Quippy Quill, including Michael Murray, Tricia Springer, Robert Williams, and everyone else who I didn't get the privilege to speak to. Finally, thank you to all of the authors who write horror or mystery. I've been such a fan of those types of books from the moment I first learned how to read as a little girl.

CONTENTS

PROLOGUE

My fiancé, Lily, and I are asleep peacefully in bed. This foul smell creeps into my nostrils and pulls me out of my rim. Unfortunately, this smell isn't unfamiliar. The last time I smelled this awful scent was right before every character on this tv show I was watching all stopped talking, turned their heads towards me with these huge black eyes, and smiled this evil smile at me. At first, I thought it had to be part of the show, but they were looking at ME. I could feel it. I tried to turn the channel, but at every station, I flipped to, there they were. I pushed the power button to turn it off, and once I did, I turned to face this inhuman-looking creature with the same eyesas the people on TV, and I screamed! I was frozen on the sofa, unable to move or breathe.

Now here's that pungent smell once again. I look over at Lily, and she doesn't seem to notice it as she lies there, still blissfully asleep. I scan the rest of the room for anything out of the ordinary. It was hard to distinguish anything in the middle of the night. I let my eyes adjust to the darkness, and as soon as I do, I see a tall figure in the corner of our bedroom staring us down. How long was it standing there? Once Again, I'm frozen and can't move. Ireach over to wake Lily, and my arm won't budge. I try to lift my other arm or any part of my body, and I can't! I try to scream her name with everything I have, but I have no voice! No!

The figure slowly drifts closer and closer to Lily's side of the bed until he's standing over her. This can't be happening! How am I supposed to offer anyone else to this fucking demon if he won't let me speak! I try harder to get any sound out, but nothing. Suddenly, the blankets slowly slide to the floor on their own. The demon has a gigantic, vicious smile going from ear to ear. No! She starts to stir because she's now uncovered and shivers. She opens her eyes and looks over at me, and smiles. "Hey, Michael. What a you doing awake?" That smile instantly turns into a look of fear when both her legs are lifted in the air, and she has dragged off the bed, onto the floor, and out of the bedroom.

I still can't move. The door slams shut, and I'm cut off from what is happening there. All I can hear from my paralyzed state is Lily's cries and screaming for me to help her. More and more noises are coming from down the hall now, like things hitting the floor, breaking sounds, and things hitting the walls. I shut my eyes tight, clench my jaw, and try like hell to move. What have I done?!

A light shines behind my eyelids, and I open them to find a luminous glow standing over me. Now what? A lovely face appears after the light fades a bit. It's the girl I met in the store. "Amy? Aren't you the chic I met in the grocery store? What do you want? What are you? Do you affiliate with that monster out there?!" I wonder if I said that out loud. I can't speak. Did I think this to myself?

"Hi, Michael. Yeah, it's me."

I can hear her, but she's not speaking out loud. "Are we reading each other's thoughts? What's going on? I need to help Lily!"

"I'm here to help you. Yes, we are reading each other's thoughts. That way, the demon doesn't hear us. It was also me who was there that terrible night.The night Lily almost died ten years ago. That was me sitting in the cafeteria withyou. Do you remember how I tried to stop you, Michael? I tried to stop you from saying what you did in your head. You begged all that was evil to save Lily and that you would do anything for her. That deal you made was real, Michael. He ishere to collect. He wants her soul and knows you will offer yourself instead, but he doesn't want you. That's why you can't move or speak."

"Of course, I knew it was real. I knew it would work. I heard that story from my grandpa. That's how he saved my grandma's life. I have no problem dying so Lily can live."

"While that is noble of you, it is never good to make a deal with a demon. No one ever wins except for him. The only way to stop this is for you to offer your soul to me. You will become part of an everlasting team who will spend eternity fighting this in humane creature."

"What's the catch?"

"The only catch is that you will be eternal and only allowed to tell one person about your new life. You only have minutes left, Michael. Lily only has a little time. Come with me."

"Okay, okay! Just tell me what to do! I'll do anything for her!"

"Think to yourself, and only I will hear you. Just think, yes, I agree."

"Yes, I agree!" In an instant, a wave of calmness fell over me. The jaw-clenching racket stopped, and Lily came running into the bedroom. Realizing I could move again, I stood to meet her as she ran in and scooped her up in my arms. Her face was cut up and bleeding from her ears and mouth. So much rage built up inside me, but it was over. I bury my face in her long, blonde hair and breathe in the sweet smell of lavender from her shampoo. "Come on, babe, let's get you to the hospital. We'll think of an explanation for what happened on the way there."

"What did happen? That horrible thing just gave me a disgusted face and roared at me once more before he disappeared."

"It's over, my love. I'll explain everything tomorrow; let's get you taken care of right now."

CHAPTER 1

(10 years ago)

"Momma, can we please stop for ice cream? You promised we'd stop if Ididn't ask for anything."

"Honey, I'm sorry, but I am so tired, and it's getting late. Let's get some tomorrow, okay?"

"But you promised!"

"Okay, Lucas, you're right. I promised, and you behaved all day like a little gentleman. How about we hit up a drive-through for a milkshake?"

"Deal!"

My 8-year-old son Lucas and I had been doing some last-minute Christmas shopping since early that day. I was always putting things like this off till the last minute. I would always have time later; I'd think to myself. Well, later finally came on a day when I unexpectedly had my son with me. His father, whom I divorced a few years prior, had dropped him off that morning to spend the day with his new girlfriend's family. I always tried to be nice to her, but they were very different people. Some probably over a top, ridiculousparty. Her name was Liz, and she was pretty high-maintenance. Her face couldn't have been made up more beautifully. Her brand-name clothes, bags, and even sunglasses made me feel like I dressed like homeless person. I'm more of a dress-for-comfort kind of girl. However, she was always pleasant to me and friendly to Lucas, so that's all I cared about. At least I had already purchased Lucas's gifts. But he would be in for a full day of shopping, crowds, and running around.

I woke up this morning thinking that today is the day I need to get things done. Looking at myself in my foggy bathroom mirror, I take my unwashed day three hair down. Why is it that day three of dirty hair is my best day? And yet, it's the day my hair feels the yuckiest too. I throw on an old, comfy pair of jeans and my favorite oversized green sweatshirt. I put enough makeup on so I don't scare little kids and pull my long, dark brown hair into a messy yet cute bun. I say to myself, Gracie, today you will not procrastinate anymore, and you will finish all your Christmas shopping today. My full-energy yet utterly adorable son Lucas sits on the couch watching cartoons. Poor baby has no idea that he's in for a day of crowds, annoying ass people, and shopping, which is why I promised him ice cream if he went the entire day without whining for asking me to buy him anything.

As she pulls into Wendy's drive, she realizes that a frozen treat sounds perfect. "Two medium chocolate shakes, please," she says into the speaker.

She pulls up to the window to pay. They hand her the shakes and her change. She reaches into the backseat to give Lucas his well-deserved treat. He followed her all day as she went from store to store, getting last-minute gifts. He did not complain or ask for a single thing. What an amazing boy he is, she thought. Other kids would be screaming or whining about going home or enjoying a new toy. One little girl threw her fries all over the floor at the food court because they had no more ketchup—holy crap, what a little brat, she said to Lucas.

She takes her foot off the brake and accelerates out of the drive-through. Her dang spoon for the shake falls to the floor by her feet.

"Damn it," she whispers to herself. Leaning to retrieve it, she hears a passing car's horn blaring.

"Mom!"

"Sorry honey, I just dropped my spoon. There's a lesson for you when you start driving. Best not to eat ice cream and drive." I turn to the backseat and see his cute little cheeks already with chocolate shakes all over them. With his big brown eyes and blonde curls popping out of his blue beanie, I wonder how much one person can love another human being.

I need to be more careful. It was getting late. There were many holiday parties, and the weather was this horrible, misty rain. When the street seemed clear, I pulled out of the lot. There was a loud squealing sound of tires, and that's the last thing I remember.

*   *   *

Gracie awoke to lots of unfamiliar voices. The bright lights on the ceiling hurt her eyes as she felt herself being wheeled down the hallway. She then realized that she was in a hospital bed. Doctors and nurses were surrounding herbed, spitting out orders. A pounding in her head started to make her nauseous. Then she felt an ache in her side and couldn't move her left arm. The pain hits herlike a freight train all at once.

"Someone, please tell me what happened! Where is my son?!"

"I need you to calm down and take some deep breaths. Can you tell me your name?"

"Gracie Ramirez."

"Can you tell me what year it is?"

"2022. Where is my son?"

"Do you know where you are?"

"Apparently, in a hospital! Can you please tell me what the hell happened?!"

"You were in a car accident, Gracie. We have your son in another trauma room being evaluated."

"The last thing I remember, I was leaving Wendy's drive-through with my son Lucas in the backseat. I promised him an ice cream. He was such a good boy today," Gracie explained as she started to cry uncontrollably. "Please, pleasecheck on him for me!"

"He's with the doctor now, but as soon as I have any information, I'll cometo update you, okay? I promise you. Now let's get you taken care of. I'm one of the other doctors on call. My name is Dr. Hill, and I will take good care of you." He turns to his nurse and gives her some instructions. "Let's get an x- ray of the left hip, pelvis, and left arm. Also, get a head and neck CT."

I'm wheeled into a room to wait for the tech to get my films. The tech comes in and introduces herself. Honestly, I'm not even paying attention to her. She lays this board behind me and snaps a few pictures. Then she starts my IV. There's a sharp pinch in my right arm at the bend followed by the cold sensation as she starts the fluids.

"This is just the contrast solution for your CT. It may give you a yucky taste in your mouth, but it won't last long. Lay your head on this end and put your hands at your sides. The machine will give you instructions like to hold your breath when you're in there. Should only take a few minutes."

I'm thinking, yeah, whatever. As I lay back and tried to remember the events that put my son and me in the dang hospital. Afterward, they wheel me back to my room.

After what seems like forever, the doctor returns to my room. He says, "Well, Ms. Ramirez, CT looks fine, and your radiographs are good, except that you have a hairline fracture in that left arm. I will have a nurse place a cast on it,which you must wear for the next few months. I'll also have her give you something to help with the pain and to help you rest. As soon as I get more information on your son's status, I'll inform you as soon as possible."

Yeah, I'm sure I'll be able to rest when I don't know how my son is. The meds the nurse hits me with pretty fast. All I could do now was watch this annoying, mushy holiday movie they had on TV. Finally, I give in and fall asleep.

CHAPTER 2

(Present Day)

"Thank you, have a good one," says the barista as I grab my to-go eggnog latte. I had just enough time before work to stop for coffee, which I desperately needed. At least it was Thursday, which is our Friday. The dental office where I've worked as a dental assistant for the past fifteen years is closed on Fridays. That three-day weekend is a luxury most places don't have.

I see Lisa, the other dental assistant, walking across the parking lot toward me with her vast purse and gallon water jug in her arms. Lisa has been working here a lot longer than I have. She and I are very similar. Both of us are very organized and control freaks, with maybe a splash of OCD. Both are short in height with dark brown, curly hair. She and I love to have a drink together on Thursdays afterwork after a long week. The two of us clicked quickly.

"Morning, Lisa," I say as I walk in.

"Ugh, morning slut, and I see you have coffee. Why don't I see one in my hand?"

"Because I don't like you, you whore," I say with a smile. Did I forget that we both have a weird sense of humor?

Lisa and I start our morning routine by preparing for the day. I show her the schedule. "It's gonna be a hectic day, dude.

"Yeah, for sure. Lots of toothaches, which means lots of surprises." She makes an annoyed face at me. "It'll make the day go by fast though."

A day full of toothaches is the worst in our world. Never know how the day is going to go. It could be nothing, could be an easy fix or a referral, or it could be a lengthy procedure that's going to make us run behind all day. But no matter the day, I loved my job and couldn't see myself doing anything else.

I work at a privately owned dental office with a fantastic group of people. Not to mention the best boss ever. There's one general dentist/owner, three dental hygienists, and two dental assistants, Lisa and myself. I'm lucky to have a great group of people to work with. They aren't just co-workers; they're my closest friends. Not to mention a great support system. This time of year is always the hardest for me. While most people love Christmas music, shopping, and overly sentimental holiday movies, I fall into a deep depression. They do what they canto distract me and cheer me up. I put on my best fake smile and try to play along. So many bad things have happened in my life. And even though I feel very blessed where I currently am, it's hard not to sometimes dwell on the past.

"Morning, Dr. Bailey," I say as a boss man walks in with sizeable black coffee. Dr. Bailey is only two years older than me. He's married with three young boys. Most of us there have children. This makes him very understanding when it comes to leaving early or needing the day off because of a child's situation. He can also be a good listener when it comes to almost anything. He also doesn't over treatment plan and screw patients over with work they don't need; he does an excellent job, and all his patients adore him.

"Morning Gracie, morning Lisa. How are my two favorite pain in the asses?" He asks with a smile.

"Oh hahaha, Mr. funnyman today, huh." We all have an odd, funny sense of humor. Pretty much everyone in our office has one. Sage, our front desk girl with octopus arms the way she can multitask, walks to the back with the first patient's chart.

"Sharron is going to be a few minutes late. She got stuck at the train." Sage says after she puts the chart in the bin. Sharron is our office manager.

"Okay,who wants the first patient's chart?"

"I'll take it," I say as I reach for the chart bin.

"Well, it's a new patient, and she seems kind of freaky."

"Why's that?"

"You'll see when you get her back. I don't know what it is, but she gives me the damn creeps."

"Well, let's start this morning off right then, shall we," I say as I walk out to the waiting room. "Mrs. Torres, I'm ready for you."

This older woman sitting in the corner slowly turns her head toward me. She grabs her cane and stands up. She follows me to the operatory, and I help her sit in the patient chair.

"Hi, I'm Gracie, and I'll be helping Dr. Bailey and you today. Want to tell me what's going on?" All she does is stare straight ahead with this eerie blank expression. "Ma'am, are you in any pain? What is it we can help you with the day?"

"He's coming."

"I'm sorry. Who's coming?""He's coming."

"Mrs. Torres, is someone coming here to be with you?""He's coming. He's coming. He's coming."

She stops and turns her head towards me. Her eyes are black and look dilated. We lock eyes for what seems like several minutes. She grabs my wrist and smiles the most significant, scariest smile I've ever seen. My heart is beatinga mile a minute, and I can't feel my legs. What is wrong with this lady?

"It's almost time, Gracie."

"Time what for?"

She brings my wrist up by her mouth, smiles even more significantly, and bites down hard.

CHAPTER 3

(10 years ago)

I wake up to my right arm being squeezed to death by a blood pressure cuff. "What the..."

"Sorry to wake you. How you feelin'?"

"Where's Lucas?"

She does a quick once over on me. "How's your pain level?"

"I'd be better if I knew how my son was. I can handle a little bruising and a broken arm."

"I'll go get Dr. Anderson. She's been your son's doctor. I believe she's about to take him up to surgery."

"Surgery?!"

"Let me see if I can get one of her nurses or fellow to talk to you, okay? But I can tell you this; she is one of the best pediatric surgeons in the country. Lucas is in good hands."

She leaves my room, and I'm left with all my thoughts. All my worries. This doesn't seem real. Just a few hours ago, we were shopping and getting ice cream. Now all the things I'm usually stressed about, all my insignificant problems, seem like nothing. I feel like I'm holding my breath as my mind goes a mile a minute

*   *   *

After what feels like a lifetime, the nurse returns to my room with another doctor.

"Ms. Ramirez, I'm Dr. Anderson. I am the doctor who operated on Lucas. My team is taking him to recovery as we speak."

"I need to see him. Please take me to see him now!"

"There are some things I need to go over with you first. I must prepare you for what's about to happen and how Lucas will look when you see him. He had apunctured lung, a broken femur, a few broken ribs, and a subdural hematoma, which is a brain bleed. We had to insert a rod in his femur to repair it. He won't be able to walk on it for a while. We also had to insert a chest tube to help him breathe. You will also see that the top part of his head is wrapped. We had to perform a craniotomy to stop the brain bleeding. There was a great deal of swelling in the brain. We had to remove a section of his skull to allow the brain room to swell. I know this is a lot, but I want to prepare you. There is no way to tell the deficits he will have when he wakes up or if he will wake up at all. We have him in the ICU and will monitor him closely. Before I take you there, do you have any questions?"

"What do you mean you don't know if he'll wake up?"

"I wish I could tell you more, but at this point, we've done everything we can for him. All that's left to do is wait. I'll bring you up there now."

They wheel me to his room. It feels like the longest ride of my life. I have this huge lump in my throat, and I can barely open my eyes because they are so swollen from crying. I can't breathe. This has to be a dream. This can't possibly be happening to my son. I pray that maybe there's a chance they have the wrong boy. Perhaps somewhere in this hospital, Lucas is just sitting and waiting for me.This has to be a mistake.

They wheel me next to his bed. It was hard to digest what I saw. I picked up his little hand and squeezed it. He didn't squeeze back. His head was bandaged,he had a tube coming out of his mouth, and not to mention all the bruises on his cute little face.

"Lucas, I'm here, honey. It's hard even to get words out. Momma is right here, and I'm not going anywhere. I am so so sorry, sweetheart." I bring this tiny hand up to my lips and give it a kiss as more tears roll down my splotchy cheeks.

"Ms. Ramirez, his brain activity has been decreasing. I'm very sorry, but it's not looking good. If it continues to decrease and gets to nothing, it means he will need all these machines indefinitely to keep him alive. We will continue monitoring him throughout the night, but you may want to call family or friends to come to be with you. Again, I'm very sorry, Gracie."

The doctor leaves the room, and a nurse enters. "Hi, I'm Marie, the nurse on call tonight. I'll bring you a pillow and blanket to rest in that chair. If you need anything else or have questions, push that button."

"I need my phone, but I'm unsure where it is."

"There is a bag of your belongings I was told was left in your room. I'll run and get it for you."

"Thank you." She leaves, and I'm left alone, holding my baby's hand. Then the tears started, and I knew they would never stop.

CHAPTER 4

(Present Day)

Her eyes stayed locked on mine. "Ma'am, you're hurting me! Let go!" She would not let up. Her black eyes seemed to get even darker. As her teeth squeezed harder and harder, she looked still smiling through all those yellow teeth. The pain was growing more intense, and I started to bleed. Blood is dripping down my hand and onto the floor.

"Ma'am, let me go! Now! Let go! Let go!" I'm screaming this over and over again, and yet no one seems to hear me. People keep walking on by like they don't even see what's happening. Can they not freakin hear me! Do they not even see me? Finally, Dr. Bailey walks in. "Thank goodness! Please get her off of me!"

"Good morning, Mrs. Torres. What's going on today?" he says after giving me a weird look.

She lets go and turns her head towards him. Her eyes are now normal the way they were before. "Hello, doctor. I have this tooth on this side that has been driving me nuts. It is hard for me to even chew on this side." She opens and points to a tooth in the back of her mouth. Her teeth, which were all pointy and yellow a minute ago when they were gum deep in my flesh, are now just old lady looking.

I glance down at my wrist which was just bleeding and shaking in pain, is also normal again. No blood, no teeth marks, no pain. What in the actual hell just happened? Did I imagine the whole thing? I stand there with tears in my eyes and hold my wrist, unsure of anything.

"Gracie, are you okay?" Dr. Bailey is looking at me like I've lost my mind.

"Um, yes. I'm not feeling great. Can I be excused? I'll send Lisa in here."

"Yeah, that's fine." He turns to that psycho freak of a lady and starts looking in her mouth. "Okay, let's see what's going on here."

I go down the hall and find Lisa rinsing instruments in the sink. "Hey, can you go in there with him? I'm dizzy. I'll sit in the back for a few minutes.

"Yeah, sure. Are you okay?

"Yeah, I'm fine. It could be because I skipped breakfast. I'll be fine."

*   *   *

"Ugh, what a long ass day. My feet are killing me." Lisa heads to the back to change out of her scrubs.

"Yeah, mine too." I follow her back there to get my stuff too. I still don't know what the hell happened today.

"So, how you feelin'?"

"I'm good, just so ready to get out of here. It's been a long week."

"Alright, well, go home, have a beer, and try to get some rest."

"Sounds like a plan. I'll see you. Have a good night."

"You too, girl."

We lock up and head to our cars. She parks up front, and I park around theside usually. Reaching for my keys at the bottom of the abyss of my big, oversizedpurse, I look back toward the building. Standing halfway between there and my car is a dark figure. I squint my eyes because I'm unsure what I'm looking at. Is that an actual figure of a person, or just a shadow from the bushes or something? The harder I stare, the more it doesn't look like just shadows. "Lisa?" I scan the parking lot for Lisa. Maybe she forgot something inside and is heading back in. Her car is gone. I need to get out of here.

My hands are trembling, and I drop my dang keys. I squat down and frantically search the ground for my keys. I stand up and hit the unlock button on the keys in hand. Then I see it in the reflection of my car window. I'm frozen. I glared at myself with the most sinister smile I'd ever seen and eyes that were vast and black. It slowly opens its mouth and lets out a horrible, ear-piercing scream. No human could make a sound like that. I'm too scared to run or open my door.I cover my ears, shut my eyes, and start to pray. I pray until my heart starts to calm and my breath finally slows down. With fear and courage, I open my eyes. It's gone. I need to get home.

CHAPTER 5
(10 years ago)

I'm not sure how my phone wasn't destroyed in the wreck, but I'm glad it wasn't. However, it'd be even better if none of this happened at all. I scrolled through my contacts for the number. I don't know her number by heart, but who does now a days? "Hey, mom, it's me. Please come to St. Mary's hospital. Lucas and I were in an accident. I'm okay, but Lucas isn't doing well." I give her a brief run down of everything. When we hang up, I turn my attention back to Lucas.

Seeing him lay there so helpless reminds me of him as a baby. He would sleep so soundly with those long eyelashes and cute little nose. I put my fingerin his little chubby hand, and he wrapped those tiny fingers around mine. But my baby isn't there. My hand is holding him, but he doesn't hold mine back. I lay my head down on his bed. My eyes start to burn like I'm about to cry, but nothing comes out. I think I've cried so much that I have nothing left. I begin to drift offto sleep.

Later that night, the door swings open, and it startles me. "I'm here, honey."It's my mom. She comes over and hugs me. Yep, there are my tears again.

"Mom, thank God you're here."

"Why didn't you call me sooner?" She puts my face in her hands.

"We need to pray."

"The chapel is down the hall. But I don't want to leave his side, mom."

"No baby, that's not what I mean. There's another prayer we need to say. We need to make a deal, and I need you to trust me completely if you want Lucas to live. Can you do that?

*   *   *

My family has always been a little superstitious. Seriously, I don't need this right now. I grew up in a modest home in San Antonio, Texas. It was myself, my younger brother Ray, my mom Teresa, and my aunt Julie. My aunt Julie moved in when my dad, Joseph, died when I was 17. I was two years older than my brother, but we grew up close. I felt protective over him. I considered him my best friend, just as my mom and aunt Julie were. We lived in a quiet subdivision where everyone seemed to know everyone. There were block parties and backyard barbecues all the time. Ray and I grew up with all the kids on our street.

One afternoon, my parents invited some neighbors over for a pool party. I loved weekends like this. My dad would cook sausage and burgers on the grill, my mom and aunt would make cupcakes, and everyone who came by would bring something different—so many yummy things to eat. Most of them had kids our age. The boys brought their water guns over for war, while the girls brought their barbies. I loved to play barbies. We would put their swimsuits on, too, and they would have their pool party.

Our backyard was like a dream. When you walk out the back door, there'sa covered area with two ceiling fans, outdoor tables, and a vast smoker/bbq pit. Surrounded by a metal fence was a lagoon-shaped swimming pool. It had a big rock waterfall with a flat top. Perfect for climbing up and doing cannon balls off of. Of course, my brother and I could not jump off without our water wings, eventhough I could swim on my own. I was an excellent diver and sometimes pretended to be diving in the Olympics. I'd dive, and everyone would cheer. The water wings, however, would not let me under the water for more than a second before I'd pop back up. So annoying.

With so much going on at once, no one noticed that Ray started climbing the rock to jump. "Hey! Watch this!" he yells. But with all the adults in conversation, only some look over. "Mom, can I show you I can jump without my floaties? Pretty please!"

She looks over and gives him a wave and a smile. She didn't hear what heasked. I look back toward Ray in time to see him pulling off his water wings. "Ray, no!" I yell.

"Mom said I could.""No, she didn't!"

"You're not the boss, Gracie!" He holds his nose and jumps in.

"Mom! Dad! Ray jumped in without his wings!" Unsure if anyone heard me scream, I swam over to where he went under. With the chlorine water stinging my eyes, I can see him at the bottom, struggling to return to the top. He's making a climbing motion with his arms but getting nowhere. As I pop my face back up, I see my dad running over and jumping in.

"Gracie, come out of there! Everyone out of the water now!" my mom yells.

I scramble out of the water and run over to my mom. She scooped me up in her arms and hugged me tight.

"Mom, I told him not to. I tried to stop him. I'm sorry, mom." I put my face deep into her neck and started to cry.

"Don't you dare, baby? It's not your fault. I should have paid more attention." Now she's crying too.

The pool is cleared as everyone circles and watches my dad pull Ray's limp body out.

"Someone call 911!" shouts my dad.

"Already got them on the line! They're on their way!" shouts back James. He's one of our neighbors who's friends with my dad.

My dad lays Ray on his back, listens for breath or a heartbeat, and begins CPR. Time seems to stand still. After a few rounds, he lowers his ear back to his chest. Guess he hears nothing because he starts again. This pattern seems to go on for what seems like forever.

Finally, the sounds of sirens flood the street. My dad doesn't stop, though. Three paramedics burst through the back gate. One carries a duffel bag, and the other brings a stretcher. The one who had the bag takes over for my dad. It's hard to see my brother lying there like that.

"How long has he been down?"

"About 10 minutes," answers James. Once, I saw him dive in to get him. I called. My phone said I was on the phone with 911 for 10 minutes.

As one continues compressions, another guy takes this machine out and puts these stickers on Ray's chest and side. "Clear!" His whole body convulses. I turn back away from everything. I can't stand to watch this.

"We are going to get him to Memorial Hospital. You can ride with us, and the others must follow us. Does he have any allergies?"

"No, no allergies." my mom says as she grabs her keys. "You go with them, Joseph. Gracie and I will follow."

"I'll drive ya'll!" my Aunt Julie yells. "You're in no condition to drive."

We run to the car, and we pull up to the hospital before I know it. We see them pulling the stretcher with my sweet baby brother on it. Once inside, things move pretty quickly. I don't remember a whole lot after that. I do recall sitting on my dad's lap. He held me tight and rocked back and forth while he cried. My mom and Aunt Julie went somewhere, I think, to pray. The two of them and my grandmother have always been very religious. Not that I wasn't. My brother and I went to church and bible study even when we were tiny. But they were a little extra. Some stuff they seemed more secretive about. Like if you talk ugly about someone, it comes back on you. Or if you don't do the sign of the cross before you drive onto the highway, you will crash.

They get back to the waiting room to join me and dad. This other young guy with light brown hair walked by us, gave my mom a sad look, shook his head, and walked away. Who was that? They give each other a strange look before they sit. I remember that because I thought it was weird. A doctor enters the room shortly after.

"Mr. and Mrs. Ramirez, I'm Dr. Stevens. We were able to resuscitate him. He is awake and seems to be responding well. He smiles at them as he walks backout. There don't appear to be any deficits. For as long as he was down, it's a miracle he's alive. This is the first time I've seen something like it. We want to keep him here for a few days, but it looks like he will be okay. Excellent job withthe CPR, Mr. Ramirez."

Aunt Julie turns to mom and quietly says, "See, I told you it works."

CHAPTER 6
(Present Day)

Ugh, what a strange freakin day. All I want to do is to shower the day off of me, pour a huge glass of wine, lay on my couch, and watch an old movie. Plus,for it being Houston, it sure has been cold lately. Even though it's December, it's usually still warm out. Searching through my collection of recorded movies, I settled on this romantic comedy. It is the corniest movie ever, but I needed it then.Tilting back my head, I finish my glass, lay down, and finally drift off to sleep on the couch.

I wake up because of my phone's constant, annoying dinging. Why did I fall asleep on the couch? My neck is seriously sore. Every joint in my body pops as I sit up. Wow, fourteen missed text messages. It's a group text I'm in with all of my co-workers. I started to skim them. Oh yeah, shoot. Tonight is game night. It's a bunch of who will bring what for snacks, drinks, and stuff like that. Crap, it's already 1:00 pm. How did I sleep in so late? Guess I was more tired than I realized. I reply to the group.

Okay, so it's BYOB, and I'll bring my buffalo chicken dip. I type as I rub the sleep out of my eyes.

Well, look who finally chimed in!

Are you hungover already, girl? Lol I hope you can handle it tonight.

I'm not hungover, guys. I just caught up on some sleep. Guess I was tired as fuck. Lol!

You're going to have to remind me how to play Bunco.

Seriously dude! How many times have we played?!It must be your old age!

Yall are too much :)

I'll see yall tonight bitches!

Okay, see yall tonight. Remember, 6:00 pm, my house.

I realize I have nothing I need to make my buffalo chicken dip. I need to run to the store for that stuff and definitely more wine to bring over. After I brush my teeth and throw on a bra and some shoes, I head to the store.

With my basket loaded with wine and dip ingredients, I head to the checkout line. I unload my cart onto the belt and then search for my wallet. I needto get a smaller purse. It's a tote bag that I thought was so cute but way too big. It's a dang bottomless pit of crap. If I had a smaller bag, I wouldn't have had time to look up and see that scary-ass whatever I saw last night. I heard the cashier say something but didn't quite catch it. "I'm sorry, what?"

"Who's it going to be, Gracie?"

"Who's what going to be?"

"It's almost time. I need a soul."

I stare at her for a second. Her eyes look like they are now dilated and black. Time seemed to stop as we stared at each other. No, no, not again. That's what the crazy lady looked like at work yesterday. I can't seem to catch my breath and start to sweat.

"Ma'am, you okay?"

"No, no, no." I say quietly

"Ma'am?" The cashier looks scared to death and looks at me like I'm crazy.

"Um...I'm so sorry. I refocus and snap out of it. What did you say?"

"I asked if you're using cash or a card."

"Oh, card." I swipe my card, grab my bags, and leave there quickly. Seriously, what the hell is going on with me? Am I losing my mind? Poor girl will probably be freaked out for the rest of her shift.

I sat in my car for a few moments to gather myself. Okay, shake it off, Gracie. Get your shit together. My stomach starts to growl; something awful. Maybe I need to eat.

Pulling up to the drive-through of this burger place, my legs still feel weak after what happened in the store. I order a cheeseburger and curly fries. Figure I should eat something heavy if I'm going to be drinking tonight. As I pull up to pay, my cell phone rings. Ugh, it's my mom.

"Hey, mom, how are you?"

" Hey, my Gracie poo! What are you up to today?"

"Gracie poo? Mom? Why do you still insist on calling me that?"

"I don't care how old you are, Ms. Thing! You'll always be my Gracie poo,and as long as I am your mother, I will call you whatever I want. Ha Ha!"

"Fine, have it your way," I smile. "I'm just grabbing a bite to eat; then I have game night with the girls from work."

"Oh, okay. I would like to make dinner for you soon. I want to talk to you about something."

" Is everything okay, mom?"

" Yeah, I'm okay. Just let me know when you're free. I'll invite your Aunt Julie too. I'll make your favorite. I'll do some teriyaki chicken, fried rice, steamed broccoli, and homemade rolls. How's that sound?"

"That sounds amazing, mom. I can do next Tuesday at about 6:30. Does that work?"

"Yeah, that works. I'll see you then. Love you!"

"I love you too, mom. I'll see you soon."

The guy at the window hands me my bag of greasy deliciousness, and I head home. My mom can be strange and annoying sometimes, but I know she means well. I smile to myself, thinking about happy she makes me. She would always do anything for anyone. I seriously couldn't ask for a better one. She hasn't had the easiest life. First, my kid brother almost drowned in our pool when we were kids, then about ten years later, my dad died in a horrible car wreck. Yet through all of that, she stays strong.

I arrive back home and get everything unloaded and inside. I leave out the bottle of wine I'm bringing tonight and put it aside. While letting the oven preheat to 325 degrees, I combine my buffalo chicken dip ingredients in my glass pan. Once I have it in the oven, I set a timer; I need to shower and get ready.

Heading downstairs, I order an uber driver on my app. Get-togethers with those girls can tend to get a little crazy. Best not to drive home.

A car pulls up to the driveway, and a really cute guy gets out. "Hi, I'm Ryan. Are you Gracie?"

"Yes, that's me. Thanks for getting here so quickly. It's so cold out here." Glad I brought my oversized jacket. I'm sure I'll warm up as soon as I get a little wine in me. I texted the group chat to let them know I was on my way. We drive silently for a few minutes, which is always awkward with getting an uber. It makes me uncomfortable, but I know it's not their job to entertain me while getting me to my destination.

"So, has it been a busy day for you?" I ask.

"Oh yeah, it's always busier with all the parties and stuff during the holidays. It's safer than people drinking and driving, though."

It's starting to get hot in his car. He has the heater on, but it doesn't look like it's on that high.

"Um, excuse me, but please turn down the heater?" I ask as we pull up to a red light. He doesn't seem to hear me. "Hey, it's getting boiling in here. Can youturn the heat down just a little?" Still no response. The light turns green. We sit there for another few seconds, and the cars behind us start to honk. One goes aroundus, giving himthefinger and yelling something out of their window. What the heck is this guy's problem? I take my seat belt off and lean forward. Okay, so he's not asleep or freakin dead, which is a relief. His eyes are wide and staring straight ahead. The light turns red again. This is making me nervous. "Hey," I say as I put my hand on his shoulder. "Are you okay?"

He turns his head to the side to face me and lets out this horrible, ear- piercing scream! I'm stuck when I try to remove my hand from his shoulder. What the hell! I pull and pull, and I cannot remove my hand. I don't understand. I'm not even gripping anything. The scream seems to go on forever. My heart is racing, and my throat is on fire. That's when I noticed that was because I was screaming too. Then, all of a sudden, he stops. It's deathly silent except for the sound of my rapid breath. The light turns green again. We still don't move, but I no longer want to be in the car with him. Cars begin to honk and go around again.

"Feel the heat, Gracie." His eyes turn the blackest of black. I still can't seemto move or speak. "Can't get away, can you? You can't ever get away, Gracie. I'm coming soon." His head starts to rotate further toward me. It keeps going until his head is facing the back of the car. How is this possible? His body is still facing forward. The light turns red again. That's when his foot slams down on the gas. The tires squeal a few times before we take off. My hand is still glued to his shoulder. I look over at his face and gasp. His eyes are even wider than before and still black; his skin is now grey, and his smile goes from one ear to the other.

"Please! Please stop!" I yell. We are going so fast that I can't even see images out the window. It's all a blur. "Please, God! Please, God, help me!"

He laughs the most sinister laugh I've ever heard. "God can't help you!" We start going even faster now.

I start to cry. I shut my eyes tight and started praying in my head. The car comes to an abrupt stop. My body flies backward, hits the back seat, and jolts back forward, and I bang my head against the headrest on the driver's seat. I fall back and slump in the back seat, and the world darkens.

I awake to my name being called. "Gracie? Ma'am, we're here." Ryan is standing outside the car, holding the door open for me. "I think you fell asleep. Guess I drive pretty smoothly." He laughs as he helps me out of the car. "Well, have a good night. I'll take calls most of the night if you need a ride home."

"Um, thank you," I say to him. He gets back in his car and drives away. I'm standing there so confused about what just happened. Was all that a dream? Did I fall asleep? What the hell is happening to me?! All of a sudden, I feel something dripping down my forehead. I wipe it with the back of my hand. Its blood. I'm bleeding. I remember knocking my head on something, but did all that really happen? But it can't be, can it? Things like that don't happen in real life.

"Hey, girlie! It's Amber, one of the hygienists from work. Let's do it. Party time!"

"Hey."

"You okay? You have some blood on your forehead, dude. What happened?" She comes over, takes a tissue out of her purse, and holds it to my head.

"I'm okay. I hit on the door getting in Uber's car. I didn't think it was that bad."

"Well, it doesn't look like it's still bleeding. It must have hurt, though. Did your driver see it happen? He's responsible for that."

"No, no, it's okay. He didn't know or see me do it. I'm just that clumsy I guess. It's okay. It doesn't hurt or anything."

"Alright, well, let's get inside. It's freezing out here. Momma needs a glass of wine." She laughs and grabs my arm, and we head inside.

"About time! Where have you two whores been?" Lisa says, laughing.

"Oh, Grace and I went for dinner and drinks before arriving. We didn't want to invite you." Amber says as she makes her way to the kitchen.

"Very funny. Someone is just a jokester tonight.""You know I love you, Lisa."

"Well, of course. Everybody does."

"Ya'll are some serious goof balls," I say as I head towards the kitchen also to get a glass. Maybe I just hit my head when I got into the car. Perhaps I knocked myself out and did dream the whole thing. That has to be the only explanation. I'm just glad to be here with my friends. A night of games, drinking, and friends is exactly what I need.

Once we all have our drinks and snacks by our side, we get started with the game. The jokes, the trash talk, and the laughs are going to be limitless tonight.

"Okay, ya'll, now no cheating."

"How will we cheat at a dice game, fool?"

"Hey hey hey now!" Caitlyn says, laughing. Caitlyn is another one of our excellent dental hygienists. "With this group of weirdos, anything is possible."

"Roll! We should turn this into a drinking game." Suggests Amber while topping off her wine glass.

"We're already drinking, fools," I say as I take another sip. "That's a dangerous idea. Hahahaha!"

"I agree; let's just play the game," says Sage.

After two hours of playing Bunco, we moved the party to the kitchen. We gather around the vast island and pull up a bar stool. I grab myself another plate of snacks and a water bottle. I want to sober up a little. I could share an uber with one of the girls when we head home. They can drop me off first. I do not want to be alone with another uber driver. It doesn't matter if it was only a dream or if ithappened. After tonight, I will never ride alone in one again. I sure will if I have to volunteer to be the DD from now on.

"Hey, space cadet! What are you deep in thought about?" says Lisa, adding a few more pickles to her snack plate.

"Oh, dang. Hahaha sorry. I wonder how such a tiny person could eat so much." I say as I give her an evil smile.

"Oh, you got jokes. Since I eat so much, I'll just add your plate to my collection here." She takes my plate and pretends to eat stuff off of it.

"That's a way to lose some fingers." I slide it back in front of me. Everyone laughs like it's the funniest thing ever. "I was wondering if you want to share an uber ride home later. Figured it'd be cheaper for all of us." They all start to nod in agreement. I notice Jessica looking down at her phone. She seems irritated and sad at the same time. "What's wrong, Jess?"

She looks over at me. "It's nothing; I'm good." She's not very convincing. Caitlyn scoots over a little closer to her. They start to talk between themselves quietly. We all know Jessica's husband can be a severe dick. He never attends any of our work stuff when husbands are invited. He always talks to her so rudely.She always has to come home right after work because heaven forbid his dinner isn't ready on time. I was surprised she even came tonight. He must be out of town for'work' again. I'd bet anything that son of a bitch is cheating on her. She's told some of us a few instances of him being mean, but no telling how much she doesn't share. And who could blame her? It's not exactly a happy morning coffee conversation. I don't understand how she could put up with a guy like that. She is the absolute sweetest. But I suppose we don't understand. We don't know what goes on behind closed doors.

"We are gonna head out," Caitlyn says as she stands up. Jessica gets up aswell and takes their plates to the trash.

"Do y'all mind if I share a ride with ya'll? I'm getting pretty tired." I ask as I gather all my trash.

"Yeah, of course. I'll get the uber, and you can Venmo me yalls share later."

We should all get going. The wine is gone anyways. Plus, you guys ate all my food." That brings the last laugh of the night. Guess we are all exhausted. It was a lot of fun, though. These girls are always a blast to hang out with.

"Nite, guys. Everyone respond to the group text when you get home, so we know you got home safely."

"We will. Nite, everyone." I say as I grab my coat and purse. At least I know I'll have an uneventful ride home. Our ride pulls up, and we climb in the back seat. We smile at the driver and thank him for arriving so quickly. I look over at Jessica and notice her eyes are red and watery. "You don't have to explain anything if you don't want to, but is everything okay, Jess?"

"It's just Rick again. He's away for work but still texted me and told me I needed to go home. He looked at his phone at our security cameras and saw I wasn't home."

"So why does he need you home if he's not even there?" I ask. As soon as that question came out like a word vomit, I immediately wished to take it back. "I'm sorry. That was rude of me to ask."

"No, it's okay. He said the house looked like it was a mess. He asked how I could be out getting drunk when the house looked the way it did. He hates coming home to a messy house and will be home tomorrow. The freakin house isn't even messy. I left dishes in the sink, and there's laundry all over the couch. But it is folded. I need to put it away." It looks like she wants to cry. Why, oh, why did I ask ?"I swear he's such an asshole sometimes."

"You know we are here for you no matter what, right?"

"I know."

Caitlyn puts her arm around Jess. "She's right. We are here for whatever you need. I know it isn't our business, but why do you let him treat you this way? You don't deserve that. I know he's your husband, and you know him privately, and we don't. I know you two have been together for a long time and you love him. And we will support you no matter what."

"I get what you guys are saying. And don't think I haven't thought about leaving him more than once. I don't know if I can. He does have a good side. There are lots of times that he is just the sweetest with me. But I have seen his bad side too many times. I'm afraid of how he would react if I did tell him I was leaving."

The car pulls up to my apartment building. "Okay, guys, have a good night, and don't forget to text us, so we know you'll be home. Jess, call me if you need anything. Promise?"

"I promise. Thanks, Grace." She gives me a half smile as I shut the door. The car pulls away, and I'm left standing there alone. All of a sudden, I feel afraid again. I've been able not to think about what happened or didn't happen earlier all night. I get upstairs and flip the light on. I scan my rooms one by one. What's wrong with me? I double-check the front door to make sure it's locked and head to the bathroom. I need a long hot shower and my comfy bed.

CHAPTER 7
(10 years ago)

"Mom, I don't have time for your silly, superstitious games. I need you to be here for Lucas and me."

"Honey, I promise this isn't like that. Please do this for me. For Lucas. You know I wouldn't do or say anything to upset you. Everything I do for you comes from love. You know this." She has tears in her eyes now. I can humor her. I do know she means well.

"Fine, mom. What do you want to do too?"

"Let's go somewhere private. It'll be quick, I promise. I know you don't want to be away from Lucas for long." She leads me down the hall to a waiting area where no one is sitting. She faces me and takes my hands. She notices someone sitting in the corner of the room. Was he there a second ago? It was just this young guy wearing jeans and a white t-shirt who looked sad. "Excuse me, young man, can you please give us a minute alone?"

He comes over slowly and says, "Bad things happen, but He never gives us more than we can handle. You must have trust in him and never turn away from Him." He gives us a concerned face; and I'm not sure why, but he seems genuine.

"Um...yes, I agree, but please, I need to be alone with my daughter."

"He does give us free will, and I will respect that. Just think of what has happened in the past, and please reconsider." He walks toward the door. I turned to try and stop him from asking what he was talking about, but he was gone.

My mom faces me again. "Don't worry about that, honey; maybe he just had a bad loss or something. Now repeat after me. To all that is evil, hear me. Ineed your help."

I repeat it.

"I call upon you, Faust. Come to me."

I give her a weird look, but I repeat her.

"Don't give me that look. You have to mean this. Now repeat it three times."

I do as she says.

"Now ask him to please save the life of Lucas. You will beg this of him. You will let him know that you will be in his dept and will repay him. You have to mean it. I'm going to step outside and let you say these things. When you have finished, do not make the sign of the cross. This is all very important. Do you understand?" She stares at me with such intensity.

"Okay, mom. I got it." She leaves the room, and I shut my eyes tight. I said everything she told me to. I am still determining who Faust is. Maybe some angel. My mom has always been a woman of faith. I wanted to humor her. I walkout and give her a nod.

"You did a good thing, Gracie. Now I promise you, Lucas will be just fine."We head back to his room. How does she know he will be okay? I swear, sometimes she can just be frustrating. Not that I don't have faith, but sometimes it's just not enough.

The nurse brings us a blanket, and we pull up a chair in his room. "Don't worry, sweetie. I'm telling you it'll be okay. Now try to get some rest." My mom rests her head on the side of her chair and shuts her eyes. There's no possible way I'm getting any sleep tonight. Not when my baby is stuck in this bed. I wish I hadas much faith as my mom does, but when a doctor tells me there isn't much chance, what am I supposed to think? I hold his hand and lay my head on his bed.

*   *   *

I wake up to my mom shaking my shoulder. The blanket I covered up with last night was itchy as hell. Dang, hospital blankets seem like they're made out of fire ants. I must have been scratching all night because my arms are all red.

"Honey, wake up. Look who's up!"

My neck is so stiff that I can't even turn it. I slowly rotate, and I see Lucas has his eyes open. What the hell? "Lucas? Honey, can you hear me?" He looks over toward me and gives me a half smile. I can tell he's still in lots of pain. "Don't try to move too much, sweetie. Just stay relaxed and take some deep breaths." I turn to my mom. "Where's the doctor? Has he been here yet? Go find him or a nurse and get them in here now." She leaves the room, and I look back toward Lucas and cry. He gives my hand a slight squeeze which makes me cry even harder. I start to wonder what is left of his mind. They said he might have bad deficits if he even woke up. I need to focus on the fact that he's not dead. I hear footsteps in the hall, getting closer. Ugh, maybe I can get some answers now. The door swings open so hard it bounces against the wall. It startles me, but I look over, expecting to see my mom and the doctor standing there. No one is there. I stand up, slowly walk into the doorway, and peek outside—no sign of either of them. People are just casually walking the halls. The way the door opened, it had to be done by someone. I leave it open and sit back down. All of a sudden, the temperature in the room seems to drop. I can see my breath. I can see Lucas's breath. I know they keep hospitals cold, but damn. Then comes the smell. It was almost like a rotting meat smell. What the hell is that? I get up and start to look around the room. That smell has to be coming from somewhere. I notice something move out of the corner of my eye. I slowly turn my head toward the movement. It's the bible resting on the chair I was sitting in, and it was moving. The hair stands up on my arms, and my knees feel weak. My breathing gets faster and faster. It's still moving slowly. Suddenly, it stops. All I can hear is my breath. When I think it's over, the book flies across the room and hits the wall with a loud thud! I screamed before the doctor appeared with my mom. They stand there for a second before walking in.

"Everything okay, Ms. Ramirez?" The doctor looks at me like I'm crazy.

"I...um...yeah. I'm okay."

"Do you need to sit down?" He carefully approaches me.

"No, no, I'm fine. Can we please just focus on Lucas? I just got a little spooked. I don't know why, but I assure you, I'm fine." I slow my breathing and sit back down. My mom gives me a strange look and shakes her head at me. She walks over to sit by me and takes my hand.

"Yes, let's focus on Lucas. As you can see, he's a big smile.

"Yes, I see. I'm Dr. Lee. I'm the doctor on call. Dr. Anderson, who operated on your son, should be here soon. I'm going to do a quick neurological exam on Lucas." He smiles at him and introduces himself to him. He holds a finger up and has Lucas follow it with only his eyes, has him squeeze his hands as tight ashe can, and has him wiggle toes on both feet. Then he checks all of his incisions."Hey, there, little man. Can you tell me your name?"

"Lucas."

Hearing him say that single word, my heart skips a beat. Oh my goodness, my sweet boy is okay! This has to be some miracle! I grab his tiny feet, drop my head, and cry harder than ever. But this time, they are tears of pure joy!

"Thank you, Dr. Lee." says my mom as she shakes his hand.

"Everything looks great. After reading his chart, I don't understand why he is doing so well. Not that I'm complaining, of course. This is truly incredible. I'll have a nurse do a quick exam every hour until Dr. Anderson arrives. You can breathe now. Hug that little boy every day. I'm sure the Lord has great things planned for him." He gives us one last smile, then leaves, closing the door behind him.

"Mom, nothing else matters right now, but you wouldn't believe what happened to me right before you came here. It's the reason I screamed. There was this..." she stops me mid-sentence holding up her hand.

"Don't, Gracie. It's not the time. I know this is all hard to understand, but it connects with what we did last night. Who we prayed to. Who you prayed to. I'll explain it all more in time. Right now, let's just be happy. Lucas is alive and well. That is all that matters." She takes hold of my hand and Lucas's hand.

She's right. My son is alive—my sweet boy. My entire reason for living is still here. At that moment, that was all I needed to know.

CHAPTER 8

(Present Day)

Before I know it, it's Tuesday, and I'm heading to my mom's house for dinner. After a long ass day of being on my feet, standing all hunched over, I want a hot shower and bed. But I promised I'd still be there tonight when she texted to remind me. She does make some pretty yummy food. Plus, I'll have a good time once I'm there. I'm just tired.

As I pull into her driveway, my Aunt Julie meets me. She struts up to me in her black leggings that hug her tiny curves and a blue sweater that hangs off one of her shoulders. I swear she doesn't age.

"There's my beautiful niece! What's up! I haven't seen you in a hot minute.How are you? How's work going?" She gives me a big hug. She is the most incredible aunt anyone could ask for. I breathe in her fancy Chanel perfume.

"I'm good, Aunt Julie. Work is good too. Been busy as crap lately, but I wouldn't have it any other way. You look gorgeous as usual!"

"Awe, well, thank you, sweetie! Oh, I missed you! Come inside; it's so cold out here. Tell me more about what's been going on with you. How's that handsome son of yours? What's he doing nowadays? Doesn't he graduate this year?"

"He does, yeah. He's been busy with harder classes this year. Wants to get a head start on those college credits." I take off my coat and walk into the kitchen,where my mom has lots going on. "Damn, something smells good in here! Hi mom!"

"There's my Gracie poo!" She gives me a half hug because she's still tryingto finish the rice. "So glad you came; I thought you'd change your mind. I know how tired you are after work."

"Yeah, but there was no way I would turn down a free meal. Bahahah! Especially one of your free meals. Everything smells so so good, mom." I pull up a chair at her bar to watch her finish cooking. I've always loved watching her cook. She can multitask like nobody's business. Plus, she makes her rolls from scratch. She gets the eggs, flour, and whatever else is needed to make the dough and rolls it herself. She'll brush a little butter on top before she sticks them in the oven, making the whole house smell incredible. "Anything ready for sampling?"

"Go ahead and move the rolls off the tray, be careful. They're super hot, and I put them in my bread basket. Then you can go ahead and have one of those.I have strawberry jelly, too, if you want some." She hands me an oven mitt with cats all over it. My mom was always kind of a cat lady. It was seriously like every stray cat in the neighborhood would find her. More than likely because she fed them all. I remember her making me go outside with two plates of cat food to provide them. It was so damn embarrassing. They would swarm from every which way.

After transferring them to the basket, I smear jelly all over the top of one and eat it like there's no tomorrow. My Aunt Julie gives me the side eye. "Dang, someone's hungry."

"You can judge me all you want," I say with my mouth full of bread. "I had a long day and didn't eat much for lunch. So I will stuff as many in my mouth that I can get my hands on." I throw my head back, laughing. "You want one? Oh, that's right, you don't eat carbs. Don't worry, mom, I'll eat her share."

Aunt Julie is belly-laughing now at my nonsense. She pours herself another glass of wine. "Want some?" she asks. She holds up a bottle that is already half empty. "Oh, that's right, you have to drive home. I guess I have to drink the rest because I'm staying the night."

"Okay, now you two fools, grab a plate. Dinner is ready." Mom double- checks all of her burners to ensure they're off.

We all pull up a chair at the table after we fill our plates. We sit in silence and eat for a few minutes. Finally, mom breaks the silence. "So, how is Lucas doing in school? I'm sure he's excited about graduation."

"He's doing great. Some of his classes are earning him college credits. He wants to get a jump start."

"That's great! Tell him grandma is so so proud of him. Let him know he needs to come by and see me again soon. I want to take him shopping to get started getting him what he will need for his dorm room next year."

"Okay, yeah, I'll let him know. So on the phone last week, you said you needed to talk to me about something." I say as I walk to the kitchen with my empty plate. I should start cleaning up while she's still eating. Otherwise, she keeps me from doing anything to help. I glance over at her because it's been like two minutes at least since I asked the question. She and Julie are speaking in whispers with wide eyes. They turn towards me like they are afraid to tell me what all the whispering and worried looks are about. "Seriously, what's wrong?"

"Come sit back down, sweetie."

I cautiously sit back down. "Okay, you're freaking me out. It can't be that big of a deal."

"Do you remember the night you and Lucas were in that horrible accident about ten years ago?"

"Of course I do. How could I forget."

"Lucas wasn't going to make it, honey. The doctors had said that all that was left to do was wait. You and I went to another waiting area to pray. Do you remember? Do you remember the name of who I told you to pray to? His name is Faust. You prayed to him to save your son. You said you would be in his debt."She pauses for an eternity as I stare at her impatiently. "Well, in three days, it will be the anniversary of that prayer. I made sure to take note of the day and the time.The date was December 20th, Gracie. Tomorrow is the 17th. It is time to start considering who it will be. You didn't pray to an angel. I'm so sorry, honey, butI had you pray to a demon."

"What the hell do you mean?! You can't believe that crazy stuff, mom."

"I'm so sorry, honey, but it's true. I know it's hard to comprehend. I know it sounds crazy, but you have to believe me. Could you believe me? And honey, Lucas desperately needs you to believe me." She tries to take my face in her hands, but I wave them away. "Please don't be upset with me, Gracie. I did this for you and Lucas. His living was the most important thing. It would have destroyed you if he had died that day. It would have destroyed all of us."

Part of me wants to laugh at how beyond ridiculous this sounds. Sometimes, she can be little nuts, but this is way over the top. "Mom, I love you,but I have to go. I'm sorry, but this is crazy." I throw on my coat, grab my purse, and head to the door. Mom and Aunt Julie are following me. "I'll give you a call this weekend, mom."

"Gracie, please listen to her. By the time the weekend gets here, it'll be too late. Lucas will die." says my Aunt Julie in the most desperate voice I have ever heard from her.

"What the hell do you mean? Lucas will die." I say, spinning around to look at them.

"That's not fucking funny."

"We aren't trying to be funny." my mom says with tears in her eyes. "You asked him to save him, and in return, you would be in his debt. I didn't explain what that meant then because I knew you wouldn't take me seriously."

"Okay, great, mom. How about you tell me now what the hell that means."

"Don't speak to your mom that way! She's trying to help! If she didn't have you pray to that demon, Lucas wouldn't have made it. Please listen to her. She's telling the truth. Have I ever steered you wrong?"

I pause for a second to think. "Okay, fine." Why did I even agree to come tonight? I swear. I could be at home with my furry pink socks on, watching The Bachelor. He is giving the final rose tonight, and I get to miss it because I'm stuckhere listening to my family's fucking voodoo stories. I grab a seat on her floral sofa and take a deep breath. "Tell me everything you want me to know. I'm listening."

They sit on the loveseat opposite me. My mom closes her eyes a few seconds before starting. "Okay. The demon, Faust, is the demon you are in debt to. He saved Lucas. In exchange, you know owe him another soul. It can be anyone. You have to say aloud the exact day and time the prayer was made and who the demon can take. That doesn't sound very pleasant, but it must be done. Otherwise,he will come back for Lucas. He will take him back to hell with him honey."

"If you don't believe her, you can ask Father Alan. He can explain in more detail and give you a history of how real this is."

Mom gives Aunt Julie a nod. "Yes, he would be glad to speak with you. I'm sure he will be angry that we did this, but at least I know you trust him. But like I said, baby, time is running out. Remember, the day is the 20th.

I stand in annoyance. "Okay. I heard ya'll. I know you both believe in this stuff, but I don't. I know you'll mean well, I do, but nothing is going to happen to Lucas." I turn to head towards the door again.

My mom is off the couch and standing behind me in one swift movement."Things have been happening to you, haven't they, Gracie? Things that scare you. Things you can't explain."

The patient, the cashier, and the horrifying incident with the Uber driver. I can hear her slowly moving toward me. Halting to a stop, I freeze and feel my stomach go weak. I turn my head to the side. My voice catches in my throat, and my words are barely audible. "How do you know that?"

"Because this is what happens. He is warning you. Reminding you that your end of the bargain is approaching." She turns me to face her and holds my hands in hers. Her face changes from serious to fearful. The color drains from her face, and tears form in her eyes. "I know this because I've been through this."

"You've been through this? What are you saying?"

My mom starts to cry, and Aunt Julie takes one of my hands. "Gracie, what I'm about to tell you will be hard to hear. I need you to let me finish before getting too upset." She closes her eyes for a second and clears her throat. "Do you remember when your brother almost drowned in the pool? He went without air for a long time. When we arrived at the hospital, your mom and I entered a small room for privacy. I reminded your mom of a lesson we got from our great- grandmother. She told us about this demon when we were younger than you. We didn't think much of it and thought it was about the most ridiculous thing we hadever heard. But in that desperate moment, that was all we had. I told her that it couldn't hurt, so she did it. She made that same deal with that demon so your brother Ray would live."

I glance at mom, and she won't even look at me. Head down, staring at the floor; I can see tears hit the floor. My nose twitches, and I have this itch on my cheek. I realize I'm crying too. "Mom?"

"Don't be upset with her. Please, Gracie." After another deep breath, she continues. "When that doctor came out to tell us that Ray is alive, our knees go weak. It was just a shot in the dark that we did that. It worked. The doctor said it had to be some miracle because he was brain dead. At that moment, we were happy that Ray was alive. We didn't think about it until ten years later when horrible things began to happen. Things that are happening to you now. By the time we came to terms with what we had needed to do. "

"Hold the fucking phone." Fear and sadness are quickly replaced by rage.

"Are you about to tell me that's why my father died? Are you telling me you offered my dad to this fucking demon! Huh?! Is that what you are about to say! " My body shakes, and my face turns hot.

"My dad, who was the most incredible dad in the world, is dead because of you?!"

They desperately beg me to slow down and not walk out, but I can't be here. I can't be here with two people who are why my dad is gone. This can't fucking be! I storm out and get in my car. I can hear them yelling things after me, but I don't give a shit. I rev my engine before backing out of the driveway. My cell phone is going nuts, but it's probably just them. There's no way I'm listening to anything else they have to say.

I run upstairs, toss my purse on the couch, and just pace. Okay, Gracie, think. Is that really why Lucas lived? He was in just as bad a condition as my brother was. Is this the reason things have been frightening me? Is this why thatpatient said, 'he's coming'? Even that cashier said something similar. And that uber driver. Is that what they meant? Were those my warnings? If so, then what else is going to happen? Will this thing come for Lucas? Is he now in danger? Am I going to have to offer someone to this thing? My mind is running a mile a minute. I need to see Lucas. I ran to his room, and he was not there. I grab myp phone and try to call him. Please pick it up. Please pick it up. I get his voicemail.No, no, no. My phone dings. It's a text. Thank God, it's from Lucas. 'Hey mom, sorry I can't talk. At a friend's house, and it's pretty loud in here. Be home by 11:00. Luv you.

Okay, he's okay. I still have three days to figure this out. I need help. I needa plan. I also need to calm myself before I have a damn stroke. I decided to takea long hot shower. That may relax me a little. Relax me enough to think more clearly. I enter the steaming shower and let the hot water run over me. Leaning against the shower wall, I shut my eyes, and all I could think to do at that momentwas pray. Pray for calmness. Pray for clarity and some resolution. Pray for God to forgive me for what I've done for what my mom has done. As the scalding water starts to unwind me, I hear movement outside the shower door. My alertness spikes, and I listen intently.

There's someone, something, in the bathroom with me. I can feel it. I crackthe shower door open enough to see the whole space. My eyes scan the room intently. Nothing. I shut the door. A light clank breaks the silence, and I gasp. I rapidly wipe the steam off the shower door, so I can see without opening it again.Besides my hairbrush on the floor, I don't see anything. Guess that's what I heard.The door fogs up again to where I can't see through. I hurriedly commenced washing so I could get out of the shower. The best thing to do is to take my mom'sadvice and meet with Father Alan. He can give me some answers and my next step.

Just as I'm turning the nozzle off, something hits the door. Bang! My breathcatches in my throat, and instead of fear at this point, anger builds inside me. "That's enough! Who are you?!" Letters start to appear on the fogged showerdoor. I step back and bump into the wall. It's literally as if a finger is writing inthe steam. My body cannot move or breathe as the word 'Faust' forms on the door. I understand now that this is real. My anger intensifies and my fists shake. My entire body,for that matter, trembles. I clench my teeth together and shove the door open abruptly. "Leave us alone!" Some force pushes me onto the floor, and I hit the tile with a thud.

CHAPTER 9

(Teresa - year 2001)

"Gracie, your friends are here!" The place is a stir as I run around the house to prepare for my daughter's slumber party. Yes, my 17-year-old is havinga slumber party. It's the summer before her senior year, and she and her friends are having an old-time sleepover. They want it to be just like the ones they had when they were little. They will give each other facials, manicures, and pedicures, play board games, truth or dare, and stay up till dawn watching romantic comedies and stuffing their faces with junk food.

Gracie is my outgoing, loud one. She's insanely sarcastic, but not in a meanway. She can crack me up all day, every day. Even though she's a dance team member, doing her high kicks with that cheesy smile and bright red lipstick, she'snot so much a girlie girl. Although she plans to attend the local community college, she isn't 100% sure of her plans after graduation. I tell her that very fewpeople to know what they want to do when they grow up. I have every faith in her, though. I know she will do great things.

She runs down the stairs in a huff. "Coming!" She flies past me with her long brown hair flowing behind her. I found her some old-school onesie pajamas with feet to wear tonight. They're dark blue with little bunnies and flowers all over them. She asked for kiddie-looking jammies, and that's precisely what I gotfor her. The door opens, and there are her three best friends since middle school,also in colorful, childish pjs. "Hey hey hey! Let's get this party started, ya'll!" The herd follows her upstairs.

"The pizza is on its way, girls. I'll bring it up when it gets here.""Thanks, mom!" They disappear into her room.

"Mom, do I seriously have to listen to Gracie and her weirdo friends talk about boys and giggle all freakin night? Can I please sleep on the couch?" my son Ray asks as he grabs a soda from the frig. Ray is my younger one, about to start his sophomore year. He's my little wonder child. He loves to read and alwaysgets straight A's in school. He gets a little high-strung sometimes but wants the grades to get into law school someday. I remind him he's only in tenth grade, andI'm sure they don't look back that far, but he's determined to have this outstandingrecord. He does know how to enjoy himself, too, though. He has played baseballsince he was about ten and recently made the junior varsity baseball team with his best friend, Marcus. They also can stay up all night playing on their virtual reality game system. "Mom, I swear I won't leave my stuff all over the living room if you let me stay on the couch tonight. I promise."

"Yes, sweetheart, that's fine. You don't want to hear the giggle monsters all night. Just bring all your blankets back upstairs in the morning."

"Yes, thank you. I will."

The doorbell rings. It must be the pizza, finally. I thanked the delivery guyand took the food to the kitchen. "Come make a plate, honey, before I take the rest upstairs. You know those girls aren't going to save any for anyone. As skinny as theyall are, they can sure eat."

"When's dad getting home?"

"He had to work late but said he shouldn't be too much longer. Make him a plate, too, please."

I carry the rest of the pizza upstairs along with a few water bottles for the girls. As I walk past my room, something catches my eye, and I freeze. I hold my breath and glance back into the darkness of my bedroom. Not again. I squeeze my eyes shuttight and say a prayer to myself. There's a sinister laugh coming from a dark corner doorway. Then a door swinging open makes me jump.

"Mom, are you okay?" It was Gracie's door that opened. "Mom?"

"Yeah, sweetie, sorry. I'm fine. I just got a little startled when you opened the door. Here you go, and here are some drinks too. You, girls, have fun,and let me know if you need anything else."

"I will. Thanks, mom. Love you." She gives me her big, sweet smile and shuts the door.

Creepy things have been happening to me for like three days now. It startedwith small things. The feeling that I'm not alone when I am, hearing whispers, seeing things that can't be explained. A customer at my job yesterday was the worst so far. I am the manager of an antique shop downtown. I catch him staringat a wall display of crosses. I approach him and ask if he needs any help. He doesn't seem to hear me. Halfway through repeating myself, he turns his head back to face me and gives me the scariest smile I've ever seen. Mind you; his body was still facing forward. "Not yet, but soon Teresa. It's almost time," he says right before this ear-piercing scream. The crosses on the wall start to rotateupside down slowly one by one. I want to run away but am paralyzed in that spot. I let out ascream and shut my eyes. The shaking of my shoulder is what makes me stop. I open my eyes, and the guy looks normal again. Well, as usual as he could be after I scared the shit out of him by standing behind him screaming. And now this dark figure is in my bedroom.

I get back downstairs as fast as I can to call my sister.

"You okay, mom?" asks Ray.

"Yeah, I'm good. Do me a favor and text your dad to see if he's on his wayhome. I'm just going to be outside for a few minutes. I forgot that I told your AuntJulie I'd give her a call." I rush to the back porch because I don't want Ray to hear my conversation. Ugh, please be home, Julie, I think to myself. She answersafter two rings, thanks goodness. "Julie, are you busy?"

"Hey, sis! No, I'm not busy. Everything okay?"

"I know you didn't believe me before when I told you about these things that have happening to me. But I swear, Julie, you have to believe me! It's gettingworse. I'm starting to believe what we did ten years ago was real!"

"Teresa, seriously? Come on; you can't be serious."

"Can you just come over, please?! I'll show you. Just a few minutes ago, a dark figure was in my room."

"Teresa..."

"It spoke to me, Julie! Please just come here."

"Okay, okay! I'm on my way."

I hang up and run back inside. I don't want the kids to think something is wrong. I try to contain how sacred I am as I pace back and forth.

"Mom, dad said he's about to walk out the door. He said he had a stressfulday and couldn't wait to get home and not let all the crazy girls drive him nuts. Lol!"

I slow my breathing a little knowing that Julie and Joseph are on their way.It's all going to be okay. It has to be. There's a knock at the front door. It must beJulie because she doesn't live far and Joseph has a 30-minute drive ahead of him.I dash to the door and tell Ray to go to his room briefly. "Sorry honey, I have something kinda private to talk to Aunt Julie about." He nods and goes upstairs,stopping in the kitchen for a drink.

The door hits the wall because I opened it too hard. "Come in, come in!"

"Good God, dude! It would help if you calmed down. Come on, let's sit on the couch and figure this out." We move to the sofa, and she sits, but I can't seem to settle.

"Look, you know me, and you know I'm not susceptible to this shit, and I don't scare easy. The things that have been going on are freaking me out. If this is real, then today is the day it will hit the fan. Today is the anniversary of Ray'saccident. I spoke to grandma the other day about this, and she confirmed that it'sreal. You know grandma has a pretty level head and would NOT bullshit me! Shesaid that on this day, the demon I prayed to and made a deal with is coming for Ray unless I offer him someone else."

"Nothing is coming for Ray, Teresa. Look, you're right. Something has been scaring you. I know you, and this isn't you at all. Let's take a second and think. Have you called mom? She could help. Maybe she knows something we don't that can help."

"I'm running out of time, Julie! Today is the day, the day the doctor cameout and told us Ray is fine." I start to cry uncontrollably and can't catch my breath."I can't offer another person to him, but I will not lose Ray either." I drop to myknees in despair. I knew I wasn't crazy. What have I done?

"Teresa, look at me." She leans down and pulls my chin up to look at her."You are my sister, and I love you to the moon and back. Nothing, do you hear me? NOTHING is going to get my nephew without going through me first."

At that moment, the whole house went dark. The house is completely silent. Julie and I stare at each other wide-eyed and unable to move. Suddenly, Julie's hands are ripped from mine, and she goes flying across the room and hitsthe wall. "Nnnooooo!!" She's crumpled there on the floor with a few cuts on herface from my picture frames that fell on her after she hit the floor. I'm up to my feet in one swift motion and running to help Julie. "Julie? Julie, are you okay?"

What ... happened?"

"I'm sorry, sweetie. I'm so sorry about all of this. I have to ……"

"Have to what?"

Across the living room, at the foot of the stairs, is the exact dark figure I saw before in my bedroom. This time its face is more distinctive. While his bodyis just a huge, black shadow, his face is clear as day. On his grayish, green, scared-looking face sits a substantially wide, wicked smile that goes from one ear to theother and two ominous eyes that are black and dilated. It turns and gradually glides up the stairs. My timidness turns to complete madness, and I fly toward the stairs after it. Rotating its head to the side, it screams the terrifying scream!

"Leave him alone!" I call back at it. "What will it take for you to leave him alone, damn you!"

"Give me a soul!!" it yells in its deep voice. "Give....me.....a name!" the bass, throaty sound of its voice seemed to grab my soul and shake it aggressively.It stares at me as if waiting for a response.

My mind is fucking blank! I can't even think of what my name is at that moment. I try to think of other people who are mean or horrible. Someone the world could do without. Nothing. Nothing, nothing!! How are the kids not hearing this? This could be between him and me because the world seems to fadelike it's just us here. The sound of a car coming down the street. I gasped with a bit of relief. Oh, thank goodness! It has to be

Joseph! He'll know what to do! Hecan stop him! The car is getting closer and I see two bright headlights shining through the window. "Joseph!!" I yell, hoping he hears me.

"Joseph, it is." And just like that, the demon disappears. The lights turn back on, and the world comes back to life. I hear the girls in Gracie's room laughing, I can listen to Ray playing a video game in his room, and Julie is now standing at the bottom of the stairs looking up at me.

"Where did it go?" Julie says, rubbing the back of her head.

"I don't know." I race to the front door and scan the road for Joseph's car,but besides a stray dog digging through a tipped-over trash can and my neighborsitting on his porch smoking a cigarette, the street is empty. Where is he? I couldhave sworn that I heard his car. I saw the damn headlights for goodness sake!

All the air leaves my lungs, and the color drains from my face. No, no, no,no!! I sprint back inside as fast as my legs get me there and search for my phone.

"What? What are you doing?"

"Where's my fucking phone!"

"Mom?" Ray is coming down the stairs. "Sorry, mom, I didn't mean to startle you. I think you left your phone in the kitchen."

I scoop Ray in my arms and hug him tighter than anyone has ever embracedanother person in the history of the world.

"Um, mom...you're hurting me."

"I love you so so much, honey."

"Um...I love you too, mom."

As fortunate as I am that Ray is still here with me, I'm just as afraid that Imay have just given my husband to the demon. I have to get a hold of him before anything happens.

His phone goes straight to voicemail every time I call.

"Don't freak out yet, Teresa. We don't know anything yet."

Ray looks at us, concerned. "What are ya'll freaking out about? Earlier, dadtexted and said he was going to be late."

"Nothing's wrong, Ray. Do your mom a favor and take a trash bag to the girls. I'm sure they have a mess all over up there."

"Okay, sure."

"Come sit down, Teresa. You know how he always lets his phone freakin die before he realizes it needs to be charged. Let's try him again, and if he doesn'tanswer, maybe he's just on his way. Let's wait and see and thank our lucky starsthat that thing is gone and Ray is still okay."

I let her lead me to the couch, but I can't relax until Joseph walks throughthe door. Finally, an eternity later, there's a knock at the door. Why would he knock? Julie follows me as I seem to float to the door.

The red and blue sirens stop me in my tracks. "Sorry to disturb you, ma'am,but are you Mrs. Ramirez?"

I glare at him, not able to form words. My sister puts her hand on my back."Yes, sir, she is. Is everything okay?"

He removes his hat and asks me if Joseph Ramirez is my husband. "Yes. He's my husband. Where is he? What's happened?"

"He was in a head-on car wreck, ma'am. There was a car driving on the wrong side of the highway. We don't know for a fact yet, but I'm pretty sure the driver of that car was drunk. I'm sorry to inform you that your husband didn't survive. We confirmed his identity from the license in his wallet."

My body goes limp, and my legs give out from under me. The cop has quick reflexes and stops my fall. "Ma'am, you have my deepest condolences. They are taking him to the county hospital. We will need you to come down to identify him."

"My…my kids. I have my kids here."

"I'll stay here with them, Teresa." Julie hugs me from behind.

"Okay." I follow the cop to his car, and Julie follows behind. Before I open up the back door to get in, Julie stops me. She cups my face in her hands.

"Teresa, this...is...not...your fault. Horrible things like this happen."

I look her dead in the eye with a blank expression. "I did this, Julie. I saidJoseph's name. Now the demon has him. Don't you dare tell me this isn't my fault?" I duck my head and get in the back seat. I don't care if everyone says thatthis was an accident. Yes, things like this happen, but I know I did. I said Joseph'sname at the worst moment without thinking. All I was hoping for was that he washome. That one little word just killed my husband. That one word killed my kid'sfather. I would end myself if I didn't have kids. I must live with this horrific secretfor the rest of my life.

CHAPTER 10

(Gracie/present day)

I pulled up to St. Mary's church early the following day. I'm unsure how tostart explaining to him what's been happening. As I walk down the hall to where his office is at a swift, steady pace, I try to gather my thoughts. I wonder if he knows that my mother has also done this in the past. Even though I thought this whole thing was rubbish from the beginning, I still said those words ten years ago. Thoseexact words my mom said that saved my brother, yet killed my father—the words I said to save my son, who will claim another life in two more days. Maybe someprayer or ceremony or something can be performed to prevent this. Perhaps evenif Lucas and I hide in the church for a few days, I wonder.

Here I am, standing right outside his door. I hear papers shuffling, so I'm assuming he's in there. One final deep breath before I face the music of my stupidfucking decision-making.

"Father Alan?"

"Hello there," he says with his usual dashing smile. "Ms. Gracie, how theheck are ya?" He moves in for a hug.

"I'm sorry it's been so long since I've attended service."

"Oh no, sweetie. Life can get in the way sometimes. We get busy with oureveryday hustle and bustle. As long as you keep God in your heart, that's all thatmatters. He knows you're busy." He reaches for my hand and leads me over to his desk. "Have a seat. So, what's on your mind, Gracie? I'm guessing you have concerns about something, and it is a Wednesday morning. Are you still workingat that dental office?"

"Yes, sir. But I called in sick today because this cannot wait." I notice a pain in my palms and realize my fists are clenched so tight my nails are diggingin. "I don't know where or how to begin, so I'm just going to spit it out. Are youfamiliar with a demon named Faust?"

His smile fades, and his eyes widen. "You must never speak that name, Gracie. Where did you learn of him?"

"Originally from my great-grandmother when Julie and I were young. Webrushed it off as just being a story to scare us. I wish that it was. She told us the story of one of her old neighbors whose wife nearly died during childbirth. Her husband was a very hard and evil man. He was cruel to her. Not only did he beather physically but mentally. Her only friend was my grandma. She would come to her back door while he was at work and unload on her. She wouldn't tell us much about their conversations because they were too awful. When she becamepregnant, my grandma worried about her even more. She feared for her and her unborn child. Towards the end of her term, she heard them fighting through her window, which wasn't uncommon. But being so far along, she knew this would end horribly. There was a loud crashing sound, so she had it. She called the cops. She watched from her window as they brought her out on a gurney withthat devil-in-human form husband of hers in handcuffs close behind. Long storyshort, my grandma was approached by a doctor in the waiting room, mainly because she was the only one there for her and gave her the bad news. Not only did she lose the baby, but she lost so much blood that it wasn't looking good for her either. It broke her. She recalled a story from an older woman in her church.She made a deal with the demon, and her dear friend lived. Ten years later, she gave him her husband's name, and he died of a heart attack in prison."

"That's quite a story. But I am sorry to say, it is true. This horrible being will dangle what is most tempting to you, which can even be other things, such as great wealth, fame, youth, and power. You may get what you truly want now,but you must pay. He will come for you in ten years, and it will not be good. Evenin your most desperate times, it will never be worth it. He will win, and you willlose."

"So I've recently learned, unfortunately. My mom and aunt told me just last night that that was how my father died. It wasn't just a car wreck. It was onlymade to look like one. She made that same deal when my little brother almost drowned in our backyard pool." I pause and

lower my head in shame. "Father. " I say as my lip quivers. "I also made this deal. My son almost died ten years ago.My mom came to the hospital and convinced me to say these words that, at the time, I felt were ridiculous. I just did it to get her off my back. She wouldn't let itgo, and I wasn't in the mood with my son being so close to death. It will be exactlyten years, two days from now. Father, I've been seeing horrible things. Scary things. Something dark is coming for Lucas. It's been warning me. What do I do?Please."

His head drops to his desk, and he doesn't speak for a minute or two. Risingfrom his chair, he comes over, kneels before me, and takes my hands. He looks up at me with sad eyes. Fearful eyes. "Gracie, I'm extremely sorry. Once you getinvolved with that evil spirit, there's no going back. He will come for Lucas. Either you make peace with that and pray for God to forgive you or offer anothersoul. No human being is one to judge whether a person deserves to live or die. I will leave you with this a mother's love is the greatest of all loves. A mother will
do anything to protect her child. You cannot fight this evil being once a promiseis made. One way or another, he gets what he wants. You and your family are inmy prayers, Gracie." He stands tall above me, places his hands on my head, bows, and says a prayer.

I get up from the chair and embrace him. "Thank you, Father. Please ask God to forgive me." I grab my coat and return to my car as fast as possible. I know what I must do to protect my son. The only other way is if I find the most despicable human being I can find. And I know just where to look.

CHAPTER 11
(Lucas/present day)

Lucas awakens to the annoying beeping of his blaring alarm clock. He pulls his oversized pillow over his head with a grunt. His hand reaches out to smack it off, and is immediately regretting staying out late with his friends on a school night and, okay, *never doing that shit again.* Peeping out his bedroom door, he yells, "Mom! I'd love you forever if you made me some waffles with peanut butter on them!" When he doesn't get a response, he thinks *oh shit, I just pissed her off.* He knows how much she usually runs around in the mornings before work. Mainly because she loves to remind him when he complains aboutanything. But, of course, he loves her.

She does work hard and cooks meals for the two of them instead of just eating crap. Plus, his mom is the youngest of all his friends. She had him when she was only 21. He feels like he can talk to her about most things without her going crazy on him. She even lets him have a beer occasionally as long as he doesn't leave the house afterward. She says it's better than me doing stuff behind her back, and then I have to beat your ass. She cracks me up.

Guess she had to get to work early today. He knows he doesn't have timeto eat something and shower, but he will do both anyways.

At least today is a half day. It's the last day before they let out for Christmas break. All we are doing in every class is watching corny holiday movies today. Not that I don't like Christmas. I enjoy being invited to my friend Kenny's houseand watching his wealthy family get drunk. Pretty damn entertaining. His uncle once gave us a few beers because he thought it'd be funny. The joke was on him because we handled those babies just fine. It was a night for the books. Not that we do crazy shit all the time, but I am usually a perfect son and student,so sometimes I deserve to cut loose a little. Kenny has been my ride-or-die since before we had hair on our peaches. He has a sister, Lori, who's a year younger. I've had a thing for her for the past few months. She was always his kidsister who would try to hang with us and bring her obnoxious friends around, butlately, I've seen her differently. With her long red hair, deep green eyes, and adorable laugh, I can't help it. She wants to go to college to be a teacher eventually. She has a good heart. I shouldn't tell Kenny, though. At least not yet.The way she looks at me lately, I think she may feel the same.

I'm gonna be late, so I throw on jeans and a hoodie, grab a cherry pop tart, and scoot out the door. Ugh, it's fuckin cold out here. I fumble with my keys, and when I look in the reflection of my truck window, I see someone standing behind me. What the...I spin around, but no one is there. Um...okay, I think to myself.

Halfway to school, I hear my cell buzzing in my backpack. It's probably mom making sure I got to school okay. Walking into school, it goes off again. I take my phone out; surprisingly, it's my grandma Teresa. I swear, no matter how busy she gets or how old I get, she still worries about me. She's annoying when she hovers, but I am lucky to have a grandma like her .

"Hey, grandma. I can't talk now, but it's only a half day. Can I call you back in a bit?"

"Hey, my love, sorry to bother you. I thought yesterday was the school's last day. Well, have a good day, but yes, please give me a call after."

"Everything okay, grandma?"

"It's okay. We can talk after. I don't want to worry you when you're at school, but it is essential. I'm okay; it's not anything like that."

"Okay, sure. I'll call you right after school. Luv ya."

"Love you too, sweetheart."

Okay, let's get this day over with. I wish I could ditch today, but that would ruin my attendance record. Regarding school, I can be a dork. I want high school references and grades to get into a good college and possibly a scholarship. I hope to make lots of dough one day, so maybe my mom doesn't have to bust her ass one day. I'd love to be able to take care of her the way she has always taken care of me. After dad remarried a few years ago, I only see him on holidays and special occasions.

"Morning, kiss ass, hahaha" Kenny sits next to me in the first period.

"Kiss ass? Why am I a kiss ass?"

"Because everyone who isn't a kiss-ass is at home chilling instead of being here on this bullshit of a day."

"Okay, fine, I'm a kiss ass then. But guess you are too then, haha!"

"Hey, you know my parents will lose their shit on me if I miss another day."

"Oh, I'm sorry, buddy. Wouldn't want you to get a pow pow." His parents are cool but can be pretty strict. But then again, he has ditched a lot of school. Not enough to fail, but close enough. "I gotta take a leak, back in a sec. I wouldn't want to miss much of the exciting movie." He gives me a head shake and laughs.I raise my hand, and then I head out of the classroom.

After I do my business, I go over to the sink to wash my hands. Dang, it is quiet around here today. Guess a lot of people did skip out today.

LLLLUUUCCAASSSS

What the...did I hear my name. I turned around, thinking someone was in there. I didn't see anyone or hear anything else, so I ignore it. I grab a paper towel and hear my name again, a little clearer this time.

LLUUUCCAAS

My whole body jolts, and I spin around. What the hell? "Hello?" Nothing."Stop fucking around!" People can be so annoying. I toss my paper towel in the trash and hear my name again. This time a little louder. "Ugh! Dude seriously!

Just come out! What do you want?!" I glanced at the mirror as I turned back again and thought I saw someone standing behind me. I slowly turned to see if someone was there. Why am I freaking out? No one is there. I exhale and laugh to myself. I turn back to the mirror, where this distorted, evil face with huge black eyes is standing directly behind me.

You!!!

CHAPTER 12
(Gracie/present day)

I pull into a shopping strip so I can gather my thoughts. Okay, so our lunch break at work is at 1:00, about an hour and a half from now. My mind is going amile a minute. The first person that comes to mind is Jessica's asshole of a husband. I decided to ask her to lunch to figure out how she really feels about him. They don't have any kids yet, so I am considering offering her husband, but only if I can see how much better she would be without him. Maybe she feels trapped and more fearful every day than she lets on. I could save my son and my good friend all in one swoop. I send her a text.

Hey Jess, how's your day going?

Hey! Playin' hooky today, huh? Lol

Yeah, I stayed up waytoolatelastnightand knew I couldn't function today. Please don't tell anyone.

No worries, girl, you know I won't. What are you doing for lunch today?

I was going to run some errands. Rick wants me to make pork chops for dinner, so I must run to the store. Why?

I wanted to take you to lunch.

I'd love to, but I only have time to go to the store during lunch because he gets off the job early, so I must prepare dinner.

I can stop on the way, get what you need from the store, and meet you somewhere for lunch afterward. How about that little Mexican food place down the street from the office?

I can't ask you to do that for me.

You didn't ask; I offered. I want to talk to you about something.

Okay, dude, well, thanks. My last patient is here so I'll meet you at the restaurant after. I'll text the list in a few.

Okay, thanks, Jess

She sent the list a few minutes later. What a severe ass face! I started to wonder what would happen if she didn't have dinner ready for him when he got home. Are things even worse than they seem? Hell, maybe I have a winner here.

I run into the grocery store close to where we are going to meet for lunch and get the stuff on her list. I load her things in my trunk, get in, and start the car. Okay, I will keep the conversation casual and get her to open up. She has told me things in confidence before, but I need more. What if I can see how much she loves him and is willing to put up with his crap. You never really know what couples go through when no one is around. There may be more good days than bad. That's what I need to determine here.

I arrive a little early and get a table in the back. I ordered two glasses of water and a margarita, thinking I may need some liquid courage. A few moments later, I see her car out front. Thank goodness she came alone. I won't get much out of her with everyone around.

"Over here, Jess!"

"Hey, hooker!" She comes over and sits opposite me at the table.

"So, your second job as a pole dancer made you get off too late last night, huh? hahaha"

"Oh, let me tell you, it was a good night. Don't be surprised when I pay for lunch in dollar bills." We both get a big chuckle out of that. "So what are you gonna get?"

Glancing down at the menu, she says, "well, I can see you're drinking your lunch today, ya big lush."

"Oh, someone is just on a roll today. Trust me; momma is ordering some beef quesadillas."

"Those sound perfect."

We place our order and commence inhaling the chips and salsa. I figured we'd start with small talk so she doesn't suspect I have some motive. Once our food arrives and my margarita spreads its warmth throughout my body, I make the first move. "So, we haven't spoken much since game night last week. You were pretty upset. I don't want to upset you, but I've just been worried about you. What happened when you got home that night?"

"Gracie, I know how much you care and what a good friend you are, but I promise I'm okay. He can be an ass sometimes, but he can also be sweet. No one knows what I'm about to tell you, so please don't tell anyone."

"You know you can trust me."

"I know I can. I haven't been able to hang out after work sometimes as often as I used to because we've been going to counseling. Rick has even seen a therapist to help with his anger and control issues. He loves me, and he's trying to be better for me."

"Wow, I'm glad you told me. That's great, Jess."

"I know what ya'll think of him at work, and ya'll worry, but things are improving. When we first met, he was this unbelievably amazing guy—he swept me off my feet. He lost his job, and it took him forever to find another one. Money problems, our frustration, his drinking, and other things became too much for him. But I'm finally starting to see the man I fell in love with again." She smiles her biggest smile, and I return one to her.

"I'm so so glad to hear that. Yes, we all worry, but only because we love you."

"I know ya'll do. And I love ya'll back."

We finish our meal with talk of other things. I genuinely am happy that she will be okay, but in the back of my mind, it's apparent that I can't do this to her. We hug and say our goodbyes, and she heads back to work. I'm left alone in my car, feeling more hopeless now than before. As I sit there, I even consider offering my ex-husband. He hasn't been in Lucas's life much, so not much would change.On the drive home, I ponder that idea long and hard. I collapsed on my sofa in defeat. Even though he hasn't been the most incredible father to him, I'd be doingthe same thing my mom did. He was once an excellent dad to him. Plus, I know his family; they are good people who love him and Lucas very much. I quickly dismiss the idea, and I'm back at square one. I lay there and know how this has to end. There's no way in hell that I will let that horrible thing take my son. I'm his mother, and it's my job to keep him safe, even if I have to sacrifice myself.

CHAPTER 13

(Lucas/present)

I burst out into the hallway in a panic. Did that happen? Am I seeing shit? Maybe I'm still overtired from last night. I try to appear calm and casually stroll back into the classroom. Kenny gives me a weird look. "You okay?"

"Yeah, yeah, I'm solid." I look straight ahead and focus on the stupid movie but I can't shake this eerie feeling. I feel like everyone is staring at me, but as I glance around, no one is. Again, I hear my name being called. Something whispers in my ear. I turn in the direction of the voice, and outside the second-story window stands that same being I saw in the bathroom mirror. I push back, my desk scrapes across the floor, and now everyone is staring at me. My breathing increases, and I look around for the figure again.

"Lucas, is everything alright?" asks my teacher. "Dude, what the hell..." Kenny says, looking up at me.

"Yeah...yeah, I'm alright. I don't feel well. May I be excused?" Before waiting for my teacher's response, I grab my backpack and head to the exit. I scramble for my phone and call my grandma Teresa. Unsure why I think she can help. My grandma has always been very religious, and I know she won't think I'm a crazy person when I tell her what happened. It rings only once before she answers.

"Lucas?"

"Hey grandma, can I come by?"

"Of course, you can. You know you don't even have to ask such a question."

"Okay, I'll be there in ten."

"Something happened, didn't it?"

"What do you mean?"

"My sweet boy, I think you know exactly what I mean. Was it awful? Did something frighten you?"

"How did you know?"

"Lucas, I needed to speak with you this morning. Things are going into play, and I need to explain."

"Things? What things?"

"I'll explain everything when you get here. Please drive safely. And Lucas.....you have to trust me and believe everything I tell you."

I hang up and make my way there. I haven't said anything to my mom, but I've had intense and terrifying dreams. There's been this guy, or I think it's a guy,spying on me. He's been trying to get me to go with him. He looks a lot like the thing I saw at school today. These dreams have been vivid and scary; I'm unsure what they mean. I feel my grandma is about to explain them, though.

"Hello, my favorite boy! So happy to see you." She widens her doorway, and I go inside and sit. "Something sacred to you today, didn't it?"

"Grandma, somehow I already know you know what's been happening. Yes, I've had disturbing dreams, and today, these dreams became a reality. What or who is this dark figure, and what does it want?"

"Do you want anything to drink? Are you hungry?"

"No, ma'am. Please give me some insight on what's going on."

"Okay, my love. I will start from the beginning, and please don't interrupt me."

She tells me stories from my great-grandmother, stories from when my mom was young, and stories from when I was a young boy. It's hard to fathom. I sit there while trying to wrap my head around everything she's told me. "So, that's how my grandfather died?"

She hangs her head in shame. "Yes. As a mother, you will do anything to protect your children. I did say your granddad's name without thinking. I wasn't offering him; I was relieved he was about to be home." She starts to cry.

"Grandma, it sounds like an honest-to-God mistake. I've heard many good stories of him from you and mom. I wish I could have known him, but what happened to him wasn't your fault."

"Unfortunately, it was. I may have said his name at the absolute worst time, but if I hadn't made that deal in the first place, he would still be here."

"Yeah, but Uncle Ray wouldn't be here."

At that moment, I knew that my mom would soon face that same situation.She may not have believed grandma when she did this, but she did nonetheless. That's the reason I've been seeing this thing. It's coming for me soon if my mother doesn't offer him another soul.

"Thank you for telling me the truth, grandma. I need to get home. I needto be alone to think a way out of this."

"I wish there was a way out of this, honey. This demon isn't going to negotiate. It's evil."

"That may be, but I'm going home to do some research. There have to be other families who've gone through this. I love you, and I'll call you later." I rush out the door before she can say anything else. There isn't a lot of fucking time left.

CHAPTER 14

(Grandma Teresa/present)

Lucas rushed out of there before I could say everything I wanted. As I stand there and watch him back out of my driveway, I grasp my cross around my neck and silently pray for him. I know how much he loves his mother, and being18 now, I'm sure he feels like a man needing to protect her.

I head back inside and can't help but think about all that has happened throughout the years. I think of bringing Ray home from the hospital and watching him grow up. He is successful with a beautiful family of his own. I also think back to Lucas in the hospital and what a miracle the doctors thought he survived.My daughter was able to take her beautiful boy home. She raised him into an extraordinary man. At the top of his class, he is a polite, caring, and intelligent young man who loves his mother so much. I love watching the two of them converse.

I recall one time when Lucas was about 12 years old and worked his little tush off to earn enough money to get his mom the perfect birthday present. My daughter seriously needed a new comforter for her bed. She had this one she found at a garage sale that needed to be in better condition. As I was shopping with them one day, Gracie noticed a gorgeous queen-sized floral quilt at a pretty pricey boutique. I tried to convince her to buy it because she never spends money on herself, but she wouldn't bite. So Lucas mowed lawns, did chores for me around the house, and walked the neighbor's dogs until he earned enough to buyit for her. He handed her that quilt, and it ultimately brought her to tears.

She had him very young, and they have grown up together. This makes this whole situation ten times worse. Not that it wouldn't be horrible in the first place, but both of them would do anything to save the other. This is my biggest fear.

CHAPTER 15
(Lucas)

I rushed home, threw my stuff on the sofa, and ran to my room. I flipped open my laptop to do some research on this demon. If this is true and has happened before, there have to be others who have gone through this, and I had to talk to them. The first thing is I google Faust. Quite a few links pop up. A religious site defines him as a demon who conjugates deals with those desperatefor power, fame, wealth, and even life. In exchange, the devil will come for youand retrieve a soul in ten years' time. Depending on the type of deal, it could be the person who initiated the agreement or, if it was a deal to save a life, it comes for the person it saves unless another is offered in their place.

There was also a social media platform that presented itself. I click on it, and there are posts from many others who have experience dealing with this. I scroll through a few. There is one girl, Sara, who describes a time when her family was on welfare and barely surviving, and one day out of the blue, her mom wins the lottery. She talks about how her mother never buys lottery tickets, but there was a ticket with that week's winning numbers on her dresser. The next ten years were so amazing and filled with happiness for her family that she never questioned it. She just figured her mom got a ticket one day and won by God's grace. Then ten years later, her mother died of a brain aneurysm.

I scroll until I find a post about the same deal my mom made. Tyler describes how his father made this deal to save his life. Tyler was going throughtreatment for lymphoma. Treatments have stopped helping, and he was reaching the end. Even as a young boy, he had come to terms with his fate. He was tired of living in the hospital and knew the bills were draining his parent's savings. One day his scan magically shows that the cancer is gone. Completely and utterly gone. The doctors described it as a miracle from God. There had to be no other explanation. Ten years later, all these creepy ass things were happening. This sinister figure kept appearing to him in different ways. He thought he was going crazy until he found a note from his dad explaining everything. It stated how he had no choice and how parents would do whatever it took to protect their children. It talked about how much he loved him and how he wanted him to havea long, happy, and healthy life. He told him that one day when he becomes a father, he will understand why he had to take his own life. It also described whothe dark presence was and how he was gone now and would leave him alone.

Wow, I have to talk to this guy. I send him a private message and wait patiently for a response. Within a few minutes, my computer pings with a new message.

Hey Lucas, nice to meet you.

Hey Tyler, sorry to bother you, but I need some advice. I hate to bring up bad memories, but my mom and I are in a similar situation.

No worries, dude. It's a shitty situation, and I'll help however I can.So this demon...this is real.

I wish it weren't. I'm assuming you or someone close to you made this deal too.

Yeah, my mom. All this scary ass shit has been going on. She made the same deal to save my life; time is almost up.

Have you seen the dark figure?

Yeah, I've seen this fucker. How can I defeat him??

I wish there were a way, but this shit is accurate, and he doesn't revise deals. Trust me; I've tried. I spoke to a priest, and that was a little help. I thought my dad and I could hide inside the church until the day passed, but I couldn't find him when that day came. All I found was that note, and it was too late by then.

Do you think hiding in a church until the day ends would have worked?

I honestly don't know. Other people I've spoken to who've been through this have tried many different things to stop it, but nothing works. I'm sorry, but there's no way around it.

I have an idea. If your dad killed himself for you, I could offer myself. I can see my mom doing the same thing to save me. I'm sorry about that, by the way.

I hate you doing that, dude, but that may work. That evil thing is going to take someone no matter what. I wish I had thought of that myself. If my dad didn't leave me that note wanting me to have a happy life and shit after what happened,the guilt would have made me eventually do the same. It's hard guilt to live with,trust me.

Confirm with your mom first that that's what she has actually done that way you don't off yourself for no reason. You can find some random person to offer instead. I wouldn't say I like the idea of you doing that, and I don't even know you. However,offering to do that for your mother shows me you're a good person. I truly hope you reconsider. You'll be in my prayers.

Thank you.

I logged out and shut my computer. As I collapse on my bed, I reflect on things that have happened and contemplate what's to come. I closed my eyes and said a prayer in my head. I feel a tickle down my cheek as a tear rolls down it. I consider the idea of it being someone else instead of me, but I cannot imagine causing pain to another person. No human has the right to decide who dies and who gets to live. I have no choice. This started to save me, and it will end with me.

I lay there a few more minutes and decided to go for a drive to relax and get my thoughts together. My eyes won't seem to open. I know I'm not asleep. What the...

I try sitting up, and I can't move. It feels like a weight on top of me, holding me down. The harder I try to move, the harder this invisible force holds me down.I fight with everything I have and ask God to help me in my head. As soon as I do, the weight lifts off of me, and I gasp for air and feel a sense of relief. "Go back to HELL!!" I say as I get up from my bed. Suddenly, I'm tossed to the otherside of my room and hit the floor hard. "Fuck!"

I grab my keys and get out of there, now more angry than scared. My tires squeal as I back out of the driveway. I have a few more hours before mom shouldbe home from work, and I can only imagine what has been happening to her as they have me. Did she go to work today? Just then, I spotted her car. She didn't go to work. I park behind her. Before I turn off my engine, I look up and notice where I am. It's an insurance place. Damn it! She must have the same idea. I bet she's upping her life insurance, so I'll be cared for. Even in death, she wants to take care of me. I love her so much; I can't let her do this. I pull away quickly before she spots my car.

I arrived at the park I used to play at as a kid. Mom would bring me here most weekends. I remember her running around and playing with me, pushing me on the swings, blowing bubbles for me to chase, and even packing us lunch sometimes. Most of the other moms would sit and watch as their children played.I remember feeling so incredibly lucky to have her as a mom. I put my head in my hands and tried to stop crying. I don't want to look like a little bitch sitting byhimself crying, mainly because there's a group of guys playing basketball close by, and I don't want to embarrass myself. I can brush it off and recall other greatmoments in my life. A life I would have never been able to have at all if it wasn'tfor my mom. Part of me wishes that she had just let me go. That way, I wouldn'thave known how great life could be. Eighteen years of an extraordinary life is better than nothing. At least I'm technically an adult now, so she got to be a mother instead of having to bury her young son.

There was this one time she threw me a superhero birthday party. It was going to be awesome. She brought me this Batman costume and set the place uplike Gotham City. My friends would wear a superhero costumes too, but Batman was my favorite. It was going to be so freakin cool. Then the worst thing happened. The weather was so bad that day that none of my friends could make it. I recall sitting on the sofa with my costume on, and mom tried to cheer me up.She said driving in was too bad, and we could reschedule it. I knew she meant well, but I was way too upset. The next thing I know, she comes out of her room with her face all painted up like the Joker. She had two nerf guns in her arms andtossed me over one. We chased each other around the house and played all afternoon.

I should get home. I can't see mom telling me what's going on, so I shouldn't let on that I know. I'll give her a lovely evening since they are now limited. Walking back to my car, I notice a guy standing alone in the parking lot. He gives me a big smile as he casually walks over to me. "Um..hi there. Sup dude, can I help you?"

"I was wondering if there's any way I can help you." He gives me another smile, and his big blue eyes almost look concerned. He is tall and has light brown,clean-cut hair, jeans, with a white t-shirt. I'm about 5 '11, and he stood at least 6 inches over me. But for some reason, I wasn't afraid.

"Why do you think I need help? Do I know you"

"My apologies. I don't mean to frighten you, but you don't know me. My name is Michael, and I know you."

"I'm sorry, but I can't place you. Look, dude, I appreciate the concern, but I'm good. You have a good one, alright." I turn and get in my car. What the heck was that about? Maybe he thinks I'm someone else. I look in my mirror to make sure he isn't still behind me, and he's gone. I scan the parking lot, but no sign of him anywhere. Whatever, there's not much weird shit that surprises me these days. I need to get home.

CHAPTER 16

(Gracie)

I stopped at a red light and tried to come up with my next move. I don't have much time left. A cardboard sign catches my eye. It's a homeless guy holding up a 'will work for food hand-drawn sign. For a moment, I consider rolling my window down, handing him some cash, and casually asking him his name. The car behind me is honking, and I realize the light has switched to green.I stall there for another second, but the car behind me grows impatient. Ugh...forget it. I speed away, annoyed. How can I even think of such a thing? That man may have a wife and children. He could even be a veteran.

Nevertheless, even if he is just a guy living on the streets because he gambled all his money away or if he's a crackhead, he is still a human being. Who am I to determine that my life is more important than his or anyone else's? I couldnever do that to another living soul.

As I turn at the light, before the damn car behind me completely loses his shit, I notice I'm about to pass by my insurance company. It may be a good idea to up my life insurance for Lucas. With me not being around, I'll still be able to care for him. He may not have his mother anymore, but at least I can go knowing he will have enough to live his best life. He can go to the college of his choice and become whatever he wants. I know he will be destroyed, but I'll make sure and leave him a detailed note explaining everything. I'm sure he won't completely understand, but I pray he will one day.

I walk inside, and it has one of those bells that sounds whenever someone walks past a certain point. "Hello?!" I look around but don't see anyone. An older woman, who looks like she has been working there since the beginning of time, finally walks out.

"Well, good afternoon Miss; what can I do for you?"

"Um, hi. I need to adjust my life insurance policy, please." I sit across from the desk, I believe, hers, because of the bifocals and many pictures of what I assume to be grandchildren.

"Of course, I'll be right with you. I am making some coffee in the back. Would you like some?"

"That's sweet, but I'm kinda in a hurry."

"Okay, dearest, give me two minutes. I'll be right with you." She heads to the back at a snail's pace.

I tap my foot impatiently and fumble with a rubber band that I take off her desk. Hopefully, this doesn't take forever; I must get home and make dinner for Lucas. I want to spend as much time with him as I can. Suddenly the thought of not being with Lucas anymore hits me like a freight train. Now that I'm doing this with the insurance, it's all becoming even more real. I wish there were another way, but I'd never be able to live with myself if I let that fucking evil demon take my son or anyone else. This is my fault, and I did this in the first place ten years ago so my son could live, and as his mother, I'm going to make sure he does.

As I wait there, I start to reminisce about Lucas's life. He was such a sweet,caring, and incredible little boy. He loved to be my little helper when I baked. He and I would have a ridiculous mess all over the counters just making cookies. Not to mention he ate more of the cookie dough than rolling it into balls. He would laugh uncontrollably at old-school cartoons that I introduced to him. I mean serious belly laughs. One night when he was about eight years old, I was lying in bed looking through all of my old photo albums because I couldn't sleep, and Lucas walked into my room and crawled into bed with me. He said he couldn't fall asleep either, so I made us some hot chocolate, and we looked at old pictures and told him stories until he fell asleep. As he grew older, we remained close. It'sbecause I had him so young. He would tell me about his first day of high school,his bad days, and even keep me up to date with all the tea. Tea is now another word for gossip.

What the heck is taking this broad so freakin long. As I stand up to go back there and check on her, I feel someone standing behind me. I freeze, and my knees go weak. There's a smell in the air all of a sudden that makes me cringe. It seems like rotten eggs or something. I lower my eyes to see what that smell could be and don't see anything. I find the courage to turn around, but there's no one back there. The scent is getting stronger, and now the hairs on my arm are standing up. My breathing increases, and my heart races. I want to yell out for the lady, but before I can, the bell goes off as if someone walked in. I can't move.

"Gracie." a deep voice whisper from behind me."Go away!!" I scream with my fists closed tight.

"Ma'am? Why the screaming? Are you alright?" the old lady comes over and gently touches my shoulder.

"I... I am so sorry. I...." I slowly sit back down and try to control my breathing. "I....I must have dosed off or something. I have bad dreams pretty often. I'm sorry. I'm good; let's just get started, please." We get down to business at last.

I shake her hand before heading out the door. I want to save time cooking,so I picked up some pizza and hot wings for dinner tonight. I pray I can get through the night without losing it. I'll need the final day to prepare myself for the following day. I need to plan everything perfectly so it'll appear to be an accident. That way, Lucas will get the money. I'll send him to his friend Kenny'shouse for the day and a sleepover. I have to get it together and remember; I'm doing this for my son, who I love more than my own life.

CHAPTER 17

(Lucas)

I walk into the house and take my stuff to my bedroom. On my way to the back of the house, I noticed the messy place. I'm sure I have time before she gets home to straighten up. There's no way I will have her come home to a shitty house.

Starting with my room, I gather all my dirty clothes off the floor to createa load. I head back to my room, scoop up all the dishes I've left there the past couple of days, and take those to the kitchen. There are still dirty dishes in the sink from this morning, so I pull up my sleeves and get to it. Damn, how long has some of the crap been in my room? I finish cleaning the rest of the kitchen,then move on to the next room. I'm usually good at doing my part, but mom does most of it. I didn't realize just how much shit she does on her own till I finally finished everything. I throw the clothes in the dryer and quickly jump into the shower.

I grab a notepad and go over to the sofa to see out the window, so I know when mom pulls in. I sat for a minute to gather my thoughts. This will be the last thing she'll ever read from me. That sinks in, and I get this sick feeling in the pit of my stomach.

Mom,

First, I want you to know that I am very thankful for what you did. Though things may not have turned out how you thought they would, you gave me a great life, and I will be eternally grateful. Please, please don't be a sad mom. I know saying that won't stop you, but think about how your life would have been if I died that night in the hospital. You would have had a breakdown and no telling where in your life youwouldbe. Just imagine that I'm off at college or something. You were the best mom a kid could ask for, from putting little notes in my lunch kit to building giant creations with me out of legos, showing up for every tiny thing I was ever involved in, and even the best superhero birthday parties. As I grew older, instead of drifting apart, we became closer. You were my mother, myfather, and my best friend. I knew I could come to you with just about anything, and I did.

Remember this one time when Kenny and I entered his parent's liquor cabinet when they went out of town? I called you because I was afraid when the room started spinning. At first, you laughed at me and said how I would feel in the morning was only the beginning of my punishment. You picked us up, replaced everything before they returned home, and nursed us the following day with that awful hangover. You did make Kenny and I practically your slaves for the next week as more punishment, but we learned our lesson. After that, even though I'd be in huge trouble, it never stopped me from coming to you with anything. I want you to promise me that you will not do anything stupid. I want the world for you, mom. If it weren't for you, I would have died when I was eight years old and wouldn't have had the incredible life I've had. I want to protect you the way you saved me. I love you more than words can even say. I will always be with you, in your memories and your heart.

Love always, Lucas

I hear her car pull up and tuck the note in my pocket. I'll hide it later in a place I know she'll find it. I wiped my face after realizing I had been crying while writing that. I don't want her to suspect anything. I stuff my feelings inside and look forward to a night of just hanging with my mom.

CHAPTER 18

(Gracie)

With my hands full, I walk in the door, and Lucas greets me. Sending me one of his amazing smiles that I love so much, he takes the food from me to the kitchen. That smile assures me he has no idea what's going on, and that's how I want it to stay till the end. "Holy cow, someone cleaned my house! It must have been little wood land creatures because my son doesn't know how to clean this good."

"I may do my little snow white whistle to call upon my furry friends; you never know. Hahaha! I got home early and decided to do something nice for you."

"Awe, that's so sweet!" I give him a big bear hug.

"Well, it was either that or hear you bitch about how I've been home for hours not doing shit. Haha!"

I give him a playful smack on the head with the now-empty paper towel roll. "How was your day?"

"It was nothing spectacular. They made us watch dumb movies in every class today, so cleaning was the big highlight of my day. How was yours? You left earlier than usual this morning."

"Um, Dr. Bailey added an early patient today, and I guess I drew the small straw." I've thought of a few things I want to say to him since I won't be here much longer. We eat silently for a few minutes before I pour myself a glass of wine. The wine will give me a little liquid courage. It has the opposite effect on me. While it can make most people in a moment like this more sentimental, it will make me brave and funny. "So tell me, have you told Kenny's lovely sister how much you like her yet?"

"No, not yet. I'm not sure how Kenny would feel yet. He would be more weirded out than upset, but I don't have the balls yet."

"Well, you should find your balls, honey." He laughs and almost shoots soda through his nose.

"Mom, please don't say balls ever, ever again." He makes a grossed-out face.

I smile and say, "I don't mean to embarrass you, but honey, I don't want you missing out on something that could be great because you're afraid. I want so many good things for you. You'll be going away to college soon, and you won'thave me around to bust your balls when you need it."

"Ugh, there it is again. But yes, mom, I get it. I was thinking of spending the night at his place tonight, so I'll make you a promise. I will tell him and Loritonight if you make me a promise in return. I want you not to be sad when I leave for college."

"That's a tough one, but you got a deal. I'll do my best anyways. I also want you to shoot for the moon in life, Lucas. Yes, do what makes you happy, but strive to be the best and find a way to make good money out of whatever it is. I want nothing but the best for you."

"We gettin' deep, huh." She gives me a face. "Okay, okay, I got it. Trust me, mom; I will always do what's right."

"I know you will." I believe him. I know he will keep up his end and havea wonderful life.

He helps me clean up the kitchen, and I can't help but stare. Stare at the sweet face I've seen go from round, baby-fat cheeks to manly stubble on his chin. The way he smiles, laughs, and even moves, I take it all in. And when I feel alittle happiness, there's that nasty smell again. Oh no, this is the same smell I smelled from the insurance office right before that thing appeared. I can't let Lucas see whatever is about to happen. "Hey buddy, I'll finish here, and you can head over to Kenny's. You've done enough cleaning for today." I hate losing time with him, but I fucking refuse to let that evil thing in the same house as my son.

"Alright, I guess I'll see ya in the morning, mom." He runs to his room to grab a bag.

I'm standing in the living room waiting on Lucas, and I notice movement from the corner of my eye. My St. Mary's figurine on the shelf above the tv, facing forward, is rotated to the wall. I walk over to it and turn it back to face thefront. As I turn to walk back towards the door, it slams against the wall in front of me and shatters into a thousand pieces. "Aagghh!" I lean back against the door, trembling. Lucas runs out of my room.

"Mom! What happened?! You okay?"

I try to control my breathing and fake a smile. "Um..yeah, sorry. I...I was going to give that to my mom for a sale the church is having, and I guess I'm clumsy."

He gives me a sly look like he's not sure he believes me. "Is there something else going on, mom? You seem a little distracted and extra in the last few days."

" I'm fine, sweetie, I promise. Have fun with Kenny tonight, and keep your promise about talking to him about Lori." I lean in and embrace him tight. I take an intoxicating whiff of the smell of his sweatshirt. It's getting harder to fight the tears, and I seriously cannot let him see me cry. As much as I want him to stay and spend as much time with me as possible, he can't be here for this. I need time to prepare. He tells me how much he loves me and kisses me on my forehead. "Ilove you too, sweetheart. Always." He walks to his car, and before I know it, he's gone. I shut the door and leaned against it for a second. How did I get myself into this?

I grab some clothes from my room and head to the bathroom. I turn the hotwater on in the shower and undress. I apply my face wash and lean over the sinkto rinse it off; the whole bathroom fills with steam. As I get the last bit of suds off my face, I splash water across my face a few extra times because the warm water feels perfect. I grab my blue hand towel and pat my face dry. I grip the towel tight in my fists and scream with everything I have. I can't regret any of this; I just can't! My son got to live and will go on to do amazing things in the world, and if I have to go to hell with this fucking demon, then so be it. I lower the towel from my face and wipe the foggy mirror. Standing behind me is this tall, dark figure with a distorted face. Its eyes are oversized and pure black. Its mouth is open wide from ear to ear, and its jaw drops to almost the middle of its chest. Behind him is nothing but darkness. My mouth drops open, but no sound comes out. Anger builds inside me, and I spin around to face it but it's gone.

I step inside the shower but leave the door open a little so that I can see out. Since my previous experience, I'm too afraid to shut it all the way. I lather myself up and rise off as fast as I can. Then, just as I shut off the water and am relieved that nothing happened while I was in there, the shower door slams shut! The door isn't budging. On instinct, I pushed as hard as I could to get out without thinking about what was waiting for me on the other side. Defeated, I leaned against the shower wall and held my breath, waiting for his next move. The bathroom is deathly silent. I can feel my heart pounding out of my chest. I squeeze my eyes tight and pray without knowing what else to do.

Suddenly, the prayer I was saying over and over in my head for the past few minutes, it seems, vanished from my brain. Our Father and I have known this prayer since I was a little girl. I start to panic. As hard as I try, the words are just gone! Just completely gone from my brain as if someone erased them! No, no, no! I shove my hands hard once more against the shower door, and as I do, the same horrible face is on the other side smiling at me. My eyes widen, and I'm shoved back against the wall before I can even scream. My head bangs the wall so hard the evil face appears blurry. I find the strength to move again, but I can't. An invisible force is holding me there, pressed to the wall. My throat starts to tighten. It feels as if a hand is around my throat, compressing it. "Agh.... no....n " I can't speak, I can't breathe, I can't move.

As I started to black out, the pressure released, and my whole body collapsed to the floor. I grab my neck and gasp for air. Once I regain strength, I reach for the sink to steady myself. My breath finally returns to normal, and I wipe my hand across the foggy mirror and notice a red hand print on my throat. I put my clothes on quickly and get the heck out of there.

I head to the kitchen for a glass of wine to steady my nerves. I set it down in the living room and decided to sleep on the sofa tonight. I don't feel safe anywhere lately, but the living room close to the front door is better than enclosed in my bedroom. After I search for a comforter in the hall closet, I locate a pen and notepad to write a note to Lucas. I want to assure him I had no choice in this.

I settled on the sofa in my pink pj set with long sleeves and little cats all over it that Lucas gave me one year for Mother's Day. He did that as a joke because I told him stories about how my mom would make me help her feed all the stray cats in the neighborhood, and I felt like the crazy cat lady.

I write about what happened on the day of our car accident when he was 8. I explained all his injuries and what the doctor said about his condition. I told him how scared I was for him and how he was my whole heart, and I couldn't bear to lose him. I hesitated for a few minutes before telling him about my deal with a demon to save his life. I tried my best to explain that I didn't know if I believed any of it but was willing to try anything. There were no other options, and letting you die was NOT one of them. I hope I made your childhood memories wonderful. Having to play the role of both mother and father, I had to be both a good cop and a bad cop. I tell him how sorry I am that he has to live the rest of his life without me. Please do not be sad for too long and keep his promises to me. I explain to him that one day when he's a father, he will know what it feels like to have unconditional love for another person. You will do anything just for them to be happy. And finally, I tell him how I will always be with him.

With tears streaming down my face, I fold the note and take it to his room.I place it under his pillow, knowing he'll find it. With a heavy heart, I returned to the sofa and lay down for the night. I try to think of all the good times and years I spent with him and how proud he made me to be his mother. Those being my final thoughts, help me to drift off to sleep with a smile on me face.

CHAPTER 19

(Lucas)

I arrive at Kenny's just in time to see Lori coming out the front door. "Where you off to?" Dang, I hope she's not leaving for the night.

She jogs up to me with a sweet smile, "Hey you. I'm just headed to the movies with a few of my girlfriends. I'll be back later."

"Sounds good. I'll be here. Invited myself over for a sleepover."

"Awe, how adorable! I think to myself, no, you're adorable. Hahaha! Well, you boys have fun, and don't let Kenny have too much to drink, or he'll wet his sleeping bag." She squints her nose and laughs again before getting in her car.

I stroll up to the front door and knock on the door quite loudly because I figure his lazy ass is probably already asleep on the sofa. The door swings open."Hey, bestie!"

"Bestie? What the hell, dude? And why da fuck you bangin on the door like you're the damn police and shit!"

I laugh and push past him. "Thought I'd come by and sleepover. My mom doesn't feel great, so I thought I'd give her some space." I lie.

"Wanna order a pizza? I'm fuckin starving." He gets on his phone to go to the website to order it.

"I already ate, but you know me, I can always eat again. Here I have some cash."

"Alright, cool. Can you listen for the door so I can scrub my ass?"

"Oh my gosh, Ken, yes, please go and do that. I'll listen for the pizza guy."

As he heads to the back, I flip on the TV. I'm flipping the channels, but I need to pay more attention to what I'm flipping through. I have to stop thinking about what is ahead and live in the moment. I can't let on to Kenny or Lori that there's anything wrong. And I promised mom I'd tell Lori how I felt about her. First and foremost, I need to run it by Kenny. He's my best friend, and if he's not okay with me telling her, then I won't. It's not like I will be around much longer to date her anyways, so if it upsets Kenny, it's not worth it. I started to debate telling her at all. What if she does like me back, and then I'm gone? I guess I'll see how tonight goes. What I do know for sure is that I have my mind made up. I'm not going to let mom do this.

I settle on a movie and go and get two plates and two sodas from the kitchen. As I put ice in our glasses, I notice movement in my peripheral vision. Iquickly turned my head but didn't notice anything that would have gotten my attention. I continue and pour the sodas over ice and hear something coming from the opposite side. I just looked. I pause and breathe because there's nothing on my other side but a wall. The noise stops, and I start pouring again. It begins again, and this time I rotate my head more apprehensively. Kenny's mom loves religious art and has several crosses throughout the house. One of those crosses on her kitchen wall is now hanging upside down. I freeze and stare at it intently.

A soft knock at the door breaks me out of my trance. I open the door, but no one is out there. I step out and look around but don't see anyone. My breathing gets super rapid, and I return inside and shut the door. The second I turn my back on it,there's another knock at the door. This time it was more complex and had three distinct knocks. I freeze again. The house is deathly quiet to the where I can't even hear any noise coming from the back of the place where Kenny was making lots of noise. Then suddenly...KNOCK, KNOCK, KNOCK! I spin abruptly and face the door. I stand there staring at the door and hear footsteps behind me. "No!"I say as I turn around.

"No, what, dude? Open the damn door." He reaches around me and opens the door. It's the pizza guy. "Alright, I'm starving. Have a good one, bro."

I peek out the door, and the pizza guy is the guy I saw at the park. He was the same tall, clean-cut guy wearing the same thing he was the last time I saw him. "Hey, I know you."

"Yes. Hello Lucas, how are you holding up?" He has a smile yet concerning look on his face.

"I... I'm fine. I'm sorry again, but I don't know who you are."

Kenny needs clarification. "Um..you know this guy or something? Hey, if you are friends, you can hang with us if you have time. Come on in and have some pizza." Kenny gestures for him to follow him.

"That's very kind of you, but I must be going."

"Okay, well, have a good one, dude." Kenny carries the pizza to the kitchen.

"Your hours are limited, Lucas. I can help you." Michael says to me after Kenny leaves.

"How do you know? Who are you?" I whisper because I don't want Kenny to hear us. "How can you help me?"

"I know about everything, Lucas. I'm here to protect you and your mother. If you voluntarily come with me, the deal is off. The catch is your soul belongs to us now. We will take care of you. However, you must join us in the fight against Faust for eternity."

"What? What do I need to do? How?"

"Yo! Lucas, shut the door, man. My mom gets mad when I let all the warm air out, and I don't wanna hear her shit." Shouts Kenny from the living room.

I look back at the guy. "My name is Michael, and all you need to do is call upon me at the deal's end, and I will come for you."

I glance back at Kenny, and he's gone when I turn back to answer him.

I shut the door and joined Kenny on the sofa. He's already put a slice of pizza on a plate for me.

"Who was that guy?"

"No one. Just some dude I met in the park the other day. Cool guy."

He nods, inhales his pizza, and reaches for another piece. We sat silently for a while, just eating and watching a movie. I can't help but think about what Michael said to me. I wanted more information, but the decision seemed like a no-brainer. At the same time, how do I know he isn't the demon in disguise? That's always a possibility, but for some reason, I trusted him. I felt safe with him. That has to count for something, right?

There's a sound of keys outside and then Kenny's dad walks in the front door. "Hey Lucas, good to see you. You guys, be sure to clean up when you're done." He gives me a smile and heads to his room.

As the movie ends, Kenny turns to me and says, "so what you wanna do now?"

"I don't know. We can put another movie on or play cards or something."

"Yeah, cards sound good. I'll text Randy and see if he wants to come by and play too. Poker is better with more people. I'll see if he knows of anyone else who will come." Randy is another buddy we've known for a long time.

"Hell yeah, the more people, the more money I can win from ya'll."

"In your dreams, dude. You can't take me on in poker. I'll smoke your ass. Hahaha!"

*   *   *

Lori walks in the front door as the game gets in full swing. "Oh dang, mom's gonna kick your ass for making a big mess out here."

Kenny mocks her then Lori shoots me a quick smile. "Mom and dad are already in bed. I'll clean up later, don't be a loser."

"A loser wouldn't take all your money in a few hands now, would they." She sits down, takes Kenny's hat, and puts it on backward.

"Alright, hey, I don't wanna hear you bitch when you lose all your 'at the mall' money."

He deals her in with the rest of us on the next hand. I love how she can be sweet, caring, and adorable and fit in with the guys too. She can talk shit with the rest of us, and that's another thing I love about her. I try not to let Kenny see me steal a glance at her.

After another hour of playing, the guys we invited headed out for the night.We all get everything cleaned up and put away. Their mom can be pretty particular, so we ensure we do well. Lori heads to the back to shower, and Kenny and I are alone again.

"You have a thing for my sister, don't you?"

I give him a surprised look. "Um..what?"

"Come one, dude. I've noticed it for a while. How come you have yet to make a move? You know she likes you too, don't you?"

"How do you know that?"

"I hear it from her all the time. She's always askin' if you're coming over, what time you'll be here, and shit like that. I asked her one day, and she admitted it. She had me promise not to say anything, though. But I see how you have looked at her the past few weeks."

"I'm sorry, Kenny. I have been looking at her differently lately, but there was no way I would make a move unless I ran it by you first."

"Hey, Lori can do what she wants, and so can you. I'm not the boss of ya'll."

"Not to get all cheesy and shit, but you're my best friend, dude, and I'm not gonna ask out your sister without checking to see how you feel about it first."

"Hey, the thought of you two as a couple is a little weird, but you're the best guy I know. I know you would do her right. I'm good with it and appreciate your wanting to talk to me first."

I give him a pat on the back, and we go back to the living room to find a movie to put on. Lori comes back with two pillows and two comforters for Kennyand me.

"Here ya'll go. I guess I'm going to head to bed." She turns to walk away, and Kenny gives me a look.

"Um, hey Lori, can I talk to you briefly?""Yeah, sure. You okay?"

"Yeah, it's nothing bad. Can we go to the porch?"

"So, what's up?" she glances at Kenny first, and he gives her a wink. Her cheeks get plush as she grabs her coat and follows me outside.

I hesitate for a minute, and not knowing how to start, I take one of her hands in mine. Her eyes get big as if she wasn't expecting that, but her features turn soft again. He doesn't take her hand away and instead gives me a smile and my hand a slight squeeze. "Um...I..I like you, Lori. I have for a while now. We've known each other since we were little, so this might be weird for you."

"It's not weird, Lucas. I've been looking at you differently, too late. You're a sweet guy."

My heart flutters, and I get this weak feeling in the pit of my stomach. I don't want to make her think we can have an actual relationship because I know I'll be leaving soon, hopefully with Michael and not a freakin demon. I contemplate how to tell her that without telling her everything. "I may be leaving soon, Lori, whether it be college or moving closer to my dad or wherever. We don't know what the future will bring, but I couldn't go any longer without telling you how I feel about you. I care about you so so much. You've become an amazing girl, and I want the best for you. Just know that no matter what life throws our way, I will always be here for you."

Her face looked a little disappointed that I didn't ask her to be my girlfriend. I hope I didn't just ruin this moment, but I can let her think I'll always be around. No matter what, though, I will find a way to look out for her. She gives me her other hand and looks up at me. "I guess with you going away soon to school or whatever, it wouldn't make sense to get into a serious relationship, huh."

"If we would have started one a while back, it'd be different. Maybe in the future but for now, I wanted you to know. I couldn't go without you ever knowing."

She touches my cheek, and I close my eyes at her touch. She leans in and kisses me on my forehead. I open my eyes, grab her chin, and gently pull her lips to mine. Her lips are soft as I always knew they'd be. Our kiss deepens, and she puts her hands in my hair. Mine lower to her thighs, and with my thumbs, I stroke the tops of them. This goes on for a few minutes, and I'm the happiest I've been in a long time. We pull back from one another and take a moment. We get up to head back inside, but before opening the door, she turns and embraces me in a big hug. I take in the flowery smell of her hair. I always want to remember this moment.

We walk in, and I shut the door behind us. "Nite, Lori."

"Nite, Lucas." She heads to her room, but not before turning to face me and giving me one last smile.

"Well, well, well, haha! So what happened? Don't tell me. I don't want to hear about your nasty mouth on my sister. Hahah!"

I give him a playful punch on the shoulder. "Shut up, stupid."

"Naw, I'm kidding. I was dozing off in here. Let's watch tv and go to sleep. Cool?"

"Yeah, I'm pretty tired too."

I spread out the other comforter on the adjacent sofa and lay down. For now, I only want to think about the last minutes with Lori and the night of fun I had with good friends. I shut my eyes and let myself drift off to sleep.

CHAPTER 20

(Gracie)

Sleep came easy at first but was broken up by horrible dreams. One was about me being locked inside a dark cell with a group of ungodly creatures who tortured me. They would pull at my hair, scratch me with their long claws, and stab me with burning hot pokers. No matter how much they hurt me, I wouldn't die. I wished and wished for death, but it would never come. I woke up soaked in sweat and panic. When I finally fell back asleep, another nightmare became even worse than the first one. I was tied up with duct tape over my mouth so tight I could barely breathe. That evil demon took turns between hurting me and trashing my house. Then, Lucas walks in and is immediately thrown against the wall. I try to speak to offer myself, but the tape is too tight. The demon laughs at me. He grabs Lucas by the throat, and after giving me one last sinister smile, the floor opens to a fiery pit below.

My cell phone ringing awakes me. I strain my eyes to see the time. The red, blurry numbers say it's only about 10:30ish. That's it? It feels like I've been asleep for hours. I reach for my phone; it's my mom. "Mom? What's up?"

"Hey Gracie poo, I just wanted to check on you. I have been waiting to hear from you since you left the house after dinner. I know you're still probably upset, but I hope you believe everything I told you. I've been so worried about you. "

"Yes, mom, I'm okay. I spoke to Father Alan, and yes, I believe you."

"I'm so sorry, honey. I hope you don't hate me."

"Of course not, mom. I could never hate you. It's because of you that Lucas is here."

"Please tell me you've found someone to offer. I know it's a horrible, disgusting thing to have to do, but I don't want to lose either of you." I hear the fear and sadness in her voice. "Please, Gracie, tell me you found someone."

"Yes, mom. I lie. I saw a homeless man the other day. I gave him money and made small talk where I learned his name."

"Okay, good. I know we aren't the ones to judge who lives and dies, but this must be done. Once it's over, it's over for good, and we can go on and forgetthis whole bad thing."

"Okay, mom. I know, and I understand. I'm going to let you go, though, okay? I'm exhausted." I try to think quickly about what to say to her to tell her how much I love her without her getting suspicious.

"You don't have to worry about me, mom. I'm going to be okay, and so is Lucas. I love you."

"Love you too, my sweet girl."

I put my phone back on my nightstand and lay back down. I try not to think about what lies ahead tomorrow, but I can't help it. I go to my closet and retrieve my photo albums. I think about the night when Lucas was little, and we stayed up late looking through these together. He was just the cutest chubby baby. I lookover almost all the pictures and get lost in all the good times until I drift back to sleep.

CHAPTER 21

(Teresa)

I hang up the phone with Gracie and have a slight sense of relief. I know this has been so hard on her, but soon this will all be over and done with. I know I won't be able to sleep well tonight, so I head to the kitchen to make some hot tea. Waiting for the water to boil, I searched for the cup that Lucas gave me one year for my birthday. It's a white mug with his picture on it. He always gave mesuch clever gifts. One year, he even gave me a plush throw blanket with many photos of the whole family.

My tea kettle lets off a whistle that makes me jump. Ugh, why does it gets me every time? I take my mug back to my bedroom and look for something on tv. Why is night time tv all trash these days? I turned the volume low and read for a bit instead. I have to have a little noise, or I can't seem to concentrate. I reach for the book on my bedside table and flip to the middle. It's one of those Chicken Soup for the Soul books I brought a few weeks ago when Gracie and I went book hunting. She loved to read as much as I did, so one day, we decided to make a day out of book shopping. I adore these types of books that have lots of stories in them. The fact that they are all real people's true stories is what gets me.

The third or fourth story I read is about a young woman who loses her husband at an early age. It gets me thinking about my husband. I know it was long ago, but I still haven't let it go. It was all my fault. I feel my eyes watering up. I set my book down and take the last few sips of my peppermint tea before calling it a night.

What was hours later, which only felt like minutes, I woke up in a cold sweat. I dreamed of that terrible night I lost my husband, and my children lost their father. I haven't had a dream like that in quite some time. It must be because I'm worried about Gracie and Lucas. How could I even let them be alone tonight? I should have asked if I could sleep over.

Suddenly, a thought hits me like a ton of bricks! I had Gracie make that deal in the middle of the night. After being observed all night, we got the news in the morning that Lucas was going to make it. Oh my God! I need to think. What time was it that we made that deal? Think! After a few minutes of scrambling my brain, I remember glancing at the clock in that waiting room we went to. It was almost 3 am. I distinctly remember because I recall thinking, *wow, that's the evil hour that we are doing this too.* I look over at the clock by my bed. It's 2:15 am!

I doubt she'll answer the phone this late, but I've got to try. I put it on speaker while rushing around to change my clothes and find some shoes. It rings and rings before going to voicemail. Ugh! I redial as I put my shoes on and run to the front to grab my keys. It again goes to voicemail. I get in the car and start the engine. I plug my phone in the car charger and say, *call Gracie* after hitting the hands-free option. No answer.

Okay, I need to get there. On the way, I think about what to do when I arrive. I have a key, so I'll just let myself in and figure it out. I know I won't be able to witness my daughter offering herself and just stand there. I should do what I should have done in the first place years ago and recite the deal myself; that way, I would be the one in this position instead. Why, oh, why didn't I think of that in the first place? And, now that I'm thinking about why I didn't, I offer myself instead of saying my husband's name back then. What kind of person amI not to even have that crossed my mind? Instead, I panicked. Well, tonight, I amgoing to right my wrongs. I pull into the driveway and turn off my car. I sit theremomentarily and think, *okay, Teresa, here goes nothing.*

CHAPTER 22

(Lucas - 1:30 AM the same night)

I'm sitting on this metal bench at the park. The sun is high in the sky withouta cloud in sight. The park is empty except for a few birds flying around and some squirrels chasing each in the branches of a tall oak tree in the center of this beautiful view. As I let my eyes take in the scene, all colors are bolder than usual. Everything is brighter and more dazzling. There's an intense aroma of flowers coming from every direction. Maybe this is heaven. I hear someone approaching and look over my shoulder. It's Michael. He sits beside me, and together we takein all the beauty surrounding us.

Michael breaks the silence after a while. "Nice here, isn't it? Peaceful."

"Yeah, it's pretty incredible. What is this place?"

"Where do you think we are, Lucas?"

"Is this heaven?"

Michael gives me a big grin. "You know, Lucas, there isn't much time left. You have a little over an hour. I can see your soul, Lucas. You are a good person. You have a heart of gold, and we could use you here. You don't want to offer yourself to Faust. It will mean a life of torture in hell, and with you gone, your mother will be going through her torture. I can help you, and your sacrifice will help others."

"What will I have to do?"

"All you have to do is commit your soul to me. The deal with Faust will be overturned. You will become immortal, and we will do our best to keep others away from him together."

"Are there others like you? And will I be able to see my family again? Not that that will change my mind, I'm just curious. There's no way I will let anything happen to anyone else because of me."

"There is that heart of gold I was talking about. Yes, there are others like me out there. And yes, you will be able to see your family still. But Lucas, we don't have much time. I need your answer. It would help if you didn't feel pressured, though. You do have free will. Your next words should come from your heart."

"Well, then, my answer is yes. I offer myself to you and want to ensure thisdoesn't happen to anyone else. You have my word." Michael shakes my hand, buthis face instantly turns from proud to fearful. I hold out my hand to him, and I feel this rush of joy at that moment. In the background, I hear singing. It's very faint, but it makes me think it is pure happiness. I know without a doubt that this was the right choice. However, the look on his face pulls me back to reality of what could be happening to my mom in the moment.

"You need to get to your mother quickly."

The next thing I know, I'm jolted from my sleep. I look around the room and remember I'm at Kenny's house. Wow, what a dream. I grab my phone and see it's about 2:15. I must get home. I look around for my shoes and keys and slipout of the house as quietly as possible.

I race down the street, hoping nothing has happened to her. I know mom, and she would not let the demon take me or offer anyone else. I pull into her driveway and see my grandma's car. She's sitting in her vehicle, gripping the steering wheel and crying.

I knock on her window. "Grandma? Grandma, what are you doing?"

She looks startled as she opens her door. "No, no! What are you doing at home? Honey, you can't be here!"

"Grandma, it's okay. Where's mom? Is she inside?"

"Yes, I think she's asleep. I've been calling and calling. We have to get in there, Lucas! I was wrong about the day; we may only have minutes left!" She runs to the front door and bangs with everything she has. "Take me! Take me, you bastard!"

CHAPTER 23

(Gracie - 2:30 AM)

Gracie is sound asleep, and Faust has been standing at the foot of her bed, staring at her for the past few hours. He knows he has her right where he wants her. She will belong to him. He turns his attention to the front of the house and turns her gas stove on. When the gas fills her home and lungs, time will be up, and she will come with me. He knew she'd offer herself. So instead of waiting, he is just going to take her instead.

Meanwhile, Teresa and Lucas are at the front door banging as hard as possible. Faust draws out the noise so she can't hear them. He heads back to Gracie's bedside and stands right next to her. His evil smell must be in her senses because she starts to stir.

Gracie is awakened by that sickening smell, opens her eyes, and sees him standing beside her. She knows her end is near and fully accepts the consequences of her actions ten years ago. Suddenly from the front of the house, she hears thesound of smashing glass which captures both of their attention. It was the sound of a window breaking. She looks back at the demon, and fear builds inside her more than ever. With the window open, all the gas will escape. He looks pissed and lets out this loud howl that shakes the whole house. Please don't let that be Lucas. He needs to stay far away from here.

She notices footsteps coming from the front towards her room. A stiffness overcomes her, and she can't move. She has no control anymore of her body. Faust has taken possession of her. She hears her thoughts plus his but has no control of her limbs. *No, no, no, please don't hurt Lucas!* She thinks that over and over in her head, knowing it won't stop him, but she has to try. Her body moves slowly out of bed and bends itself into a back bend that her body hasn't been able to do since she was a little girl. The pain is excruciating. She's sure there are a few broken bones in her back now. It has her walk like that till she gets to the doorway with her long hair dragging on the floor, pulling every time she steps. Her head lifts and spins to look at Lucas and her mom in the living room. She sees them but knows it's not her eyes they are seeing. I remember hiseyes being pitch blank and dilated. Nothing in there but emptiness. He has me peeking around the corner, glaring at them from my distorted position. I guess Lucas locks eyes with me, well, him, and it seems his eyes are adjusting to what they see. His jaw tightens, and he courageously and cautiously walks down the hall. I feel a rumble in my throat and realize I'm growling.

"Mom?" Lucas's voice catches in his throat. "Mom, he can't take control of you. The deal is over, Faust! Let her go...now."

"You think you're so smart." Faust's sour voice makes its way from my mouth. "You may have nothing to offer me anymore, but she..is...MINE!" My hands and feet carry me in the same bent over rapidly down the hall towards Lucas. So fast, both wrists are now broken, but they continue to dart me down the long hallway.

Out of thin air, this guy appears next to Lucas. There's almost a luminous light surrounding him. Then I noticed Lucas also had the same sparkle coming off of him. It's slight, but it's there. "Stop, Faust. Don't come any closer." He holds his hand up to halt me.

My body stops abruptly, and I awkwardly rise out of my upside-down stance with a vile chuckle. "Don't you dare say my name?" I spurt. Then before I realize it, I'm hurling out horrible insults toward all three of them, my mother included, who is standing close to the front door, appalled at what is going on. She is holding her cross necklace and saying a prayer. "You think that is going to save your precious daughter, you stupid bitch."

"Hey! Don't you dare speak to her that way!" Lucas shouts with an enraged tone.

I laugh even louder than before. "Putas me prohibere potes." *(You think you can stop me, in Latin)* I say to Lucas in a creepy, devilish tone that scared me to my very core.

Michael puts a hand on Lucas's shoulder. "I represent Deus." (I represent God, in Latin) "This deal is over, and you know it. I have Him on our side, and we command you back to hell, Faust."

"Fuck you! I dare you to come and take her from me! You don't have the balls, you little bastard."

Michael whispers something to Lucas, and they head toward me. They trap me in my bedroom, recite a prayer, and continue to try and cast the demon out of me. Lucas sprinkles some water on me. It must be holy water because it scorches my skin. They continue some chant and say the demon's name over and over. Something deep inside me feels agony. The next thing I know, the walls shake, and the floors vibrate beneath me. Pictures are falling off the walls, all furniture is shaking, and everything is violently being hurled around the room. My body feels like it's on fire. The demon is desperately struggling to hang on. My body is being twisted and turned in ways it shouldn't go. My hands are ripping at my hair and scratching claw marks down my face. I'm on the floor now, crying and screaming so loud that my voice is hoarse, and my throat rages with pain. I can glance up at Lucas's face; my poor son has tears in his eyes as he chants.

All at once, everything stands still, and I feel a great release. Lucas collapses over me and holds my hand. "Mom? Mom, are you okay?" He takes my other hand also, bows his head, and sobs uncontrollably. I black out.

*　　　　　　　　　*　　　　　　　　　*

I open my eyes and am blinded by fluorescent lighting and utter soreness. Lucas and my mother come into focus.

"Gracie? Oh, my Gracie poo is okay, thank goodness. Lucas! Lucas, wakeup. She's awake."

"Mom! How do you feel?"

My throat is sore, and my words are a little delayed. "I'm alive, and more importantly, you're alive." Lucas leans over and wraps his arms around my neck for a lingering hug. I can tell he's crying the way he's quivering, so I try to comfort him the best I can. I know after everything that's happened; comfort won't come easy. I rub his back as I used to when he was a little boy.

"Okay, you two, I will get breakfast from the cafeteria. Any requests?"

Lucas wipes his eyes, walks over to her, and offers to accompany her. "You want us to bring you anything, mom?"

"No, no, I'll go. I'll eat whatever breakfast I get from the nurses. It comes with my hospital bill so that I may take advantage. I watch them leave the room, lay my head back down, and try to recall last night's events. I remember bits and pieces. I know that this whole mess of a situation I put us in is over. Y'all enjoy yourselves."

CHAPTER 24
(Lucas)

Grandma and I are waiting in line in the cafeteria, and my stomach growls. I grab a cup to fill with coffee, chocolate milk, a bowl of fresh fruit, and a plate of waffles and bacon. For the first time in a few days, I feel relaxed. I feel at peace with my decision. "What'll it be, grandma? I dunno about you, but I'm starving."

"Dang, somebody's hungry. I need something to settle my nervous stomach. So much has gone on, and I'm glad it's over."

"Well, you need to eat something, grandma. Just put whatever you want on my tray, and it's on me."

She grabs a coffee, fruit bowl, and oatmeal to add to my tray as we walk up to pay. I take out my wallet, pay the guy, and we walk to an empty table.

After we sit and eat for a few minutes, I know I must talk to her. I know I'm only allowed to tell one person about my new life, and I know that will be my mom, so I'm not sure what to tell my grandma. Luckily, she doesn't ask me too much about what happened except for that other guy who showed up at the house. I just explained that he was someone I found who had been through a similar situation. We became friends, and he said he would help me in any way he could.

We finished eating and headed back to mom. Her doctor was in her room doing an exam when we arrived. "How's she doing?" I ask as I sit around down next to her bedside.

"She's doing great. Besides her wrists being broken, a few broken ribs, and lots of bumps and bruises, she'll be fine. Our plastic surgeon stitched up the scratches on her face, so the scarring should be minimal. How did this happen?"

My mom thinks quickly on her feet and explains how she got in a fight. It was quite a story she pulled out of her ass, but the doctor brought it. He wants her to stay one more night for observation but then can return home tomorrow. My grandma calls it a day, giving us both a big hug and kiss before she heads out. Now that mom and I are alone, I can tell her everything.

"Mom, I have something pretty important to tell you. I'm sure you're wondering why no one had to die at the end of this thing."

"I was wondering that. I'm so sorry I got us into this mess, but you must understand you are the most important person in the world to me. I'd rather die than lose you."

"I know, mom. You're important to me too, so after strange crap started happening, I researched. I found other stories of people who have done the samething, and knowing you; I knew you would sacrifice yourself for me." I went onto explain it all. Michael came to me in a dream and was in the park. I also explained how he was there for her and grandma's deal. He tried to stop all of them. I told her what he said to me in my dream and how I agreed to it. Mom gets this bewildered look when I tell her I'm immortal now and will spend the rest of eternity trying to stop others from doing this and battling that demon. "That's what voided the deal, mom. I had to do this."

"So that's who was there with you last night, wasn't it?"

"Yeah, that was him. You cannot say a word to anyone about this, mom. Not even to grandma. I can still live at home for a while, but as years go by, I'll have to stay out of sight because I obviously won't be aging. Promise?"

"I promise. You're an amazing person, Lucas. I knew one day you would do great things in this world. I wish I had been the one to be in this mess instead of you, though. I know this isn't the life you wanted for yourself."

"No, mom. It's okay. I can still go to college and be whatever I want. The only thing is I'd have to move every ten years or so. And I promise that I do feel pretty damn good about this. I'm going to make sure that this doesn't happen to anyone else."

We hug it out, and she seems satisfied with my response, but I know she'll always feel guilty even though she shouldn't. We hang out in the hospital for the rest of the day and watch corny holiday movies.

CHAPTER 25

(Gracie)

Lucas drives me home from the hospital the following morning. Ugh, I cannot wait to get home. I feel terrible about how my son's life will be, but at least he is alive.

We arrive home, and the first thing I want to do is shower without worrying that something is going to torture or scare the shit out of me. I let the hot water run down my face and shut my eyes. I replay the last few days in my head and try to think if there was anything I could've done differently. Then I thought back to the accident ten years ago. I guess things could have been a lot worse. Same with my brother way back when. I do wish things would have ended differently for my dad. I'm relieved this is over, and we can all move on. I am happy to have my little brother here still, though.

I get out of the shower, wrap my big grey, fluffy towel around myself and lean on the sink in front of the fogged-up mirror. I wipe it clean, knowing I won'tsee anything behind me, and smile. I take a deep breath and sigh, letting happiness sink in. I hear Lucas rustling around, probably waiting on his turn in here. I finish up real quick and head to my bedroom. "Lucas, I'm out of the bathroom if you wanna get in! Leave your clothes there because I will wash a load when you're done. I haven't done any housework with all this fighting demons and shit. HAHAHA!"

"Agh, haha! Very funny, mom." He says as he shuts the door to the bathroom.

I should call mom to let her know I'm home so she doesn't worry. I settle on the couch with hot peppermint tea and call her name on my cell. She answerson the first ring. "Hey, mom, just call in to let you know I'm home."

"Oh good, I'm so glad you are okay. I'll come by later and bring you and Lucas something for dinner. You get your rest."

"Thanks, mom. I will. Where are you anyways? It sounds like you're in your car."

"Yeah, I'm headed to the church to see Father Alan. With everything that's happened, I need more closure. Not to mention that with all I've seen, I want to feel safe and thank God for protecting us."

"I feel ya, mom. Well, give me a call when you're on your way."

"I will, my love."

"Bye, mom."

I hear Lucas rummaging around his room, so he's done. I walked into the bathroom to gather his dirty clothes. I go through his pockets like usual to ensureI don't wash anything important and come across a folded-up piece of paper. I don't like to be nosy, but this paper has 'To Mom' in front of it. I wearily unfold it as I peek around the corner to see if he's coming. I read it to myself twice. I put my hand over my heart, shake my head, and sob. My unbelievable son was going to sacrifice himself. He knew I would end up doing it and wouldn't let me. I can't believe how amazing he is. If that angel guy didn't get to him first, would I havebeen able to offer myself before Lucas did? I can't let myself think about that. What's important is that he is still here. I would love to sit down with him and this guy, though, and see what my son got into and why he didn't come to me instead. My son shouldn't have to do this; it should be me.

I go over to his room and lean against the doorway. He's lying down, staring at the ceiling, looking so peaceful. I knock on the door frame, and he looks over at me. "Hey honey," I choke out. "You okay?" I didn't realize I was crying until I tried to speak.

"Hey, mom. Yeah, I'm good. I was reflecting on everything."

I sit at the foot of his bed and hand him the note I found. He gives me his 'oh crap' look he used to give me as a kid. "I saw your car, mom. I saw it outside the insurance place, and there's no way I would let you do that."

"I'm the parent, Lucas. How do you think that would have made me feel?"

"Likewise, mom." He grabs hold of my hand and sits up. We sit and hug, and I cry until I have nothing left. How did I raise such a unique, selfless guy.

"Well, let's rest and relax the rest of the day. I'm so freakin drained. Oh, and grandma is coming by later to bring us dinner. I want to hear more about all this later, though."

"You got it, mom."

I retreat to the living room and give in to my exhaustion.

CHAPTER 26

(Teresa)

I walk through those massive wooden doors, sit in a random pew, and bow my head. I look down at my red and gold-colored rosery and run the smooth beads through my fingers, and I am thankful that my daughter and grandson are okay. There are no services today, so the church is empty, which is how I like it. I can feel safe, enjoy the quiet, and pray alone with my thoughts. I sat there for a while, grateful, but then my husband popped into my head. After that, feeling happy and grateful went to feeling sadness and guilt. I pull down the knee rest, and kneel. I placed my head on the pew before me, let the responsibility overcome me, and started bawling.

The pew suddenly squeaks next to me, and it startles me. I jump up and see a young man sitting next to me. He wore jeans and a blank white t-shirt and had the warmest smile I'd ever seen. I look at him in astonishment. I didn't hear the loud church doors make a sound, so where did he come from?

"Who are you?"

"Hi, Teresa. I'm Michael. I'm sorry I scared you. Just here to pray too."

"You look familiar. Have I met you somewhere before?"

"I was there that night."

"Oh, yes! You helped us that night. You helped Lucas save Gracie."

"Yes, ma'am. I was there and glad to help. That wasn't the first time we met, though. I've been there through it all. I tried to stop you and Gracie ten yearsago."

"What?!? What do you..."

"I was also there that night when you lost your husband. I tried to stop him,but he overcame me that night. I'm so sorry, Teresa."

"That's not funny. I don't know who you think you are, but that shit's not funny." I grab my purse angrily and stand up, but before stepping away, He reaches for my hand. I freeze, and a bright light washes over me, and I feel like I'm floating. The next thing I knew, I was back at the hospital the night Lucas was in the ICU. I'm invisible and standing in the waiting room, watching Gracie and me.I see that guy in the waiting room. He's the one who spoke to us that day right before I convinced Gracie to make the deal. That's what he was doing. He was trying to stop us. Another light flashed before me, and now I'm back in my old house, standing on my stairs. Two bright headlights beam into the living room window. From where I'm standing, I can see that evil demon standing in the driveway. From each of his eyes, two bright lights streamed into the window. Hetricked me into saying my husband's name. My husband's car was never there; he just made me think he was. No! No, no, no! I fell to my knees, and there I was, back on my knees in that church next to Michael.

"I'm so sorry to make you relive that, but I had to show you. You can't keep blaming yourself, Teresa. He knew how to get you to say anyone's name he wanted you to say, and he knew that wouldn't just hurt you but your whole family."

"How did you do that? Who are you? What are you? How do you know my grandson?"

"Your grandson is a good person. He has a pure heart, and while I can't tell you everything, I can tell you that he's in good hands. You know, He wouldn't just let anyone in here, Teresa." Then he gives her a joking laugh.

"What is your name again?""Michael."

"Well, Michael, I thank you from the bottom of my heart for giving me the closure I desperately needed. I don't know exactly what you are, an angel or something, but please look out for Lucas." Scared to touch his hand again, I placed a hand on his shoulder instead. He feels my hand resting on his shoulder and gives me a comforting smile. I bow my head, shut my eyes, and thank God. I reached down to grab my purse, and just as I was about to ask him if he wanted to go with me to pick up dinner, I looked up, and he was gone. I quickly got to my feet and glanced around. Where did he go? As freaky as that was, I wasn't afraid. A sense of peace ran through me.

Before heading out of the big, heavy church doors, I look back again and smile.

CHAPTER 27

(Lucas)

I wake up from a much-needed nap and go into the living room to look for mom. I find her lying peacefully on the sofa, sound asleep. I don't want to wake her. I'm sure she's beyond exhausted, and with all her injuries, she needs to rest and heal.

I hear a car pull up in our driveway. It must be a grandma with dinner. Hell yeah, I'm starved. I'm still allowed to swear. I think, laughing to myself. I open the door before she walks up because her hands are completely full. "Hey, grandma. Dang,that smells good, whatever that is."

"I know I'm usually against ya'll eating crap, but I thought, screw it. I brought us all some cheeseburgers and curly fries." She walks over and puts everything on the table.

After much-needed food and small talk that wasn't about horror and demons and shit, grandma heads home. Once she's gone, I turn to mom. "Hey, I know you still have many questions, and so do I. Michael is going to come by shortly and talk to both of us. Is that cool? I know you're still exhausted."

"Naw, it's okay. I need to know everything I can."

Just then, like on cue, there's a knock at the door. Yep, guess who. "Hey, Mike. I can call you Mike, right?"

"Oh, my." he laughs. "Yeah, sure. Let's all have a seat. Okay, I'm going to give you the rundown. So Lucas, like me, is immortal now. He offered his soul to us. Yes, I said to us. I am part of a group of Warrior Angels. We have all been in Lucas's shoes and chose this life instead of death for us or anyone else to be offered to that horrible demon. We are allowed to inform one person and one person only about us. So you may never tell anyone about this, Gracie. Lucas,you will spend eternity as part of an alliance. You will automatically know when Faust is near and what he's up to. We do everything we can to stop him without making a scene for humans. You will have me to help you through your first few years; then, you'll be alone. I do promise to help you, though, if you ever need me. You may go to college and live your life to the fullest. It would help if you kept in mind that you do not age. Therefore, we cannot get too attached to anyone.I am sorry for that part. I know you love Lori, and I can tell you she will be okay."

"Well, that's good to know. I can keep in touch over the phone with her and everyone else the more years that go by.

"Yes, you may. There is one more thing. Faust knows who you are. He knows your family. He will attempt to torture you and the lives of your family forever. Do Not Let Him. Keep your faith. Stay strong, Lucas, and welcome. Welcome to the team, fellow Warrior Angel."

Epilogue

"Hey, Kenny how are the kids?"

"Yo, Lucas. How the hell are ya fuckface! Why don't I see your good lookin ass around here much anymore. Too good for us huh with that fancy medical school you went to. Oh, and sorry. I should of said Dr. Ramirez. HAHAH!"

"Yeah well I don't like to hang with peasants." I laughed. "Just checking in. How's Lori? Has she had the baby yet?"

"Naw, but it should be any day now. She's fuckin huge."

"Awe come on, give her a break. That's her second baby. I'm just glad she's happy. I'll give you a shout later, bro. I gotta get back to work."

"Alright. Good to hear from ya. Hey, stay in touch man."

"I'll check in more, I promise. Later."

"Later." We both hung up the phone. Damn, I sure miss them.

I start my engine and head down the road to the deli I'm meeting mom at for lunch. It's been a while since I've been back home and my mom is about to turn 50 years old. She's aged beautifully though. I do wish she would have remarried but she seems happy. She went part time at her dental office and is now writing books. I told her years ago that she should start writing because she loved to read so much. She finally took my advice and is writing her first horror novel. I'm sure that won't be hard for her.

I grab a table seeing how I arrive first and order us some drinks. When the waiter leaves to retrieve them, I notice the woman sitting at the table in front of me has dropped her purse. She doesn't seem to notice, so I reach over to tap her shoulder. She doesn't move. "Excuse me, ma'am, I think you dropped your bag." I lean over to grab it. She turns her head to the side and I see her eyes are pure black. She doesn't say a word, just slowly rotates her head back towards me as her body stays facing forward. Her head is completely facing me now. "Hello, Lucas. Welcome home." that evil voice says to me.

"Hello there, Faust. Miss me?" I pull out my flask of holy water I kept handy and casually flick some over to him. Instantly, the face returns to normal and it's a young girl thanking me for handing her her purse. Even after all these years, I'm still not used to seeing these horrifying things. Those evil, dilated eyes that show up in unexpected places still make my heart stop and my knees weak. You never know what he's capable of.

My mom finally arrives and pulls out a chair. "Hey my sweet boy! Oh I've missed you so so much! So where it is you moved to this time?" She waves over our waiter.

"I actually just moved to Greece. It's a place I've always wanted to see. I start my new job at the hospital there in two weeks. I'm still getting settled in my new apartment. It has two bedrooms just fyi. I do wish you'd change you mind to come with me when I move."

"I think I may take you up on that this time, honey. It's getting harder and harder to live alone with that thing constantly terrorizing me. Last night, I left my computer on as I was putting the finishing touches on my manuscript, and went to make myself a snack. I came back to find a page there I didn't write. It describes how he killed my mom and how she screamed for me. It went on in detail on how he gutted her and hung her insides on her Christmas tree. Obviously she's alive and it wasn't true, but it still scared me. He is continuously knocking things down around the house and heaven forbid I have anything remotely religious in the house without it bursting into flames or just disappearing. I'm tired of living in fear thinking that one day he could hurt me or your grandma."

"Then please come home with me mom. Grandma is well taken care of by Uncle Ray and from what I understand, she hasn't had anything scary happen to her. You are the one who knows about me, so it's you and me he is going to annoy. He doesn't do things like that to me except randomly show up to try and rattle me. He is more afraid of me though instead of the other way around. I can keep him away from you, mom. You can easily be a writer anywhere."

"Sounds like a good plan to me. Give me a week or so so I can give my job a week's notice and get my affairs together." She squeezes my arm and gives me her big cheesy smile that I've missed so much. "So, how's everything going with work and with your "side job"?"

"Well I'll be the new head of pediatric surgery at one of the most up and coming hospitals in Greece. The other thing however, you know I can't talk about that. I can tell you that I have stopped that deal from happening four times since I've been doing this. Some haven't been so lucky and some I have to follow up with in the next few years. Now what do you say we grab some ice cream on the way home?"

"Another good plan. Lets just steer clear of a drive through and this time, you drive."

THE WARRIOR ANGEL

Gracie and her eight-year-old son Lucas are out doing some last-minute Christmas shopping when a nasty car wreck interrupts their night. Lucas nearly dies when Gracie's mother, Teresa, arrives at the hospital with a too-good-to-be-true suggestion. Say this prayer, and I promise your son will live. Her mother has always been very religious and quite superstitious about things. Gracie says the blessing is mainly to get her mom to drop it and be there for her and her son. The prayer works.

It's ten years later, and Gracie is haunted by something. She learns that the "prayer" she said wasn't one at all. She had unknowingly made a bargain with a demon. In return for saving her son, Gracie now owes him a soul. Either she offers one, or he will take Lucas. The closer the deal's anniversary, the scarier things get for Gracie and Lucas. Affiliations with this demon go back even further than she knew. Family secrets are coming out. She doesn't know if she wants to know. This demon will stop at nothing to get what he is owed.
How far will a mother go to save her son?

My name is Monique Beasley and this is actually my first horror book. I live in Pearland, TX with my husband of almost 20 years, my 18 year old son, and 20 year old daughter. We are both Navy Veterans who met while serving. I'm currently working as a dental assistant and have been at the same private practice for almost 15 years.

I have always been a huge fan of horror. I've been spellbound by scary movies and have been reading horror books since I first learned to read. I hope ya'll enjoy the first of many terrifying books to come.

www.ingramcontent.com/pod-product-compliance
Lightning Source LLC
Chambersburg PA
CBHW020119310726
48970CB00002B/705